D.M. Greenwood has worked for fifteen years in the Diocese of Rochester as an ecclesiastical civil servant. Her first degree was in Classics at Oxford and as a mature student she took a second degree in Theology at London University. She has also taught at a number of schools including St Paul's Girls' in London. She lives overlooking the Thames in Greenwich with her lurcher bitch. FOOLISH WAYS is her ninth clerical mystery featuring Deacon Theodora Braithwaite.

Also by D.M. Greenwood

FOOLISH WAYS

D.M. Greenwood

HEADLINE

First published in hardback in 1999 by
HEADLINE BOOK PUBLISHING

First published in paperback in 1999 by
HEADLINE BOOK PUBLISHING

10 9 8 7 6 5 4 3 2 1

ISBN 0 7472 5801 5

Printed and bound in Great Britain by
Clays Ltd, St Ives plc

HEADLINE BOOK PUBLISHING
A division of the Hodder Headline Group
338 Euston Road
London NW1 3BH
www.headline.co.uk
www.hodderheadline.com

For Nick Richens

Contents

CHAPTER ONE

Holiday Home

'You can't come in,' said the youth on the gate, all of seventeen going on twelve and a half. The Archdeacon considered for one wild moment revving his old Rover over the lad's Nikes, crashing through the barrier and ending his career in the Church of England.

'I'm here for the conference.'

The lad's eyes glazed. 'What 'frence?'

'There's a conference of diocesan workers, clerical and lay.' The Archdeacon of Medwich, the Venerable Richard Treadwell, was known for his patience. None knew how much it cost him. 'Medwich diocese,' he added to make identification easier. 'It's called "Millennial Message".' As he said it, he wished it wasn't. The lad leaned forward from the elevation of his pavement refuge beside his hut to peer into the face of this visitor from Mars in an ancient, really, really *old* car, its window wound down to reveal the tired grey face of the unrecognised dignitary.

The Archdeacon's sentence contained so many words with which the gatekeeper was unfamiliar that the boy turned to that higher authority which alone he trusted: he picked up a mobile phone, flicked an aerial from its frame

1

and clamped it between his chin and ear like a violin. This left him free to use his hands on a clipboard. Then he framed the monosyllables with which he was most at home.

'Vic? Go' a, go' a, go' a bod here wants a 'frence for a decease.'

The Archdeacon had plenty of time to observe the youth's red hair standing straight up from his head like a hogged mane, its ends, though it was difficult to be sure in the uncertain light, touched with purple. Undoubtedly there was a triad of rings in his left ear. He was slightly built and dressed in black. He wanted only a pitchfork. Across his black T-shirt in white luminescent lettering was the slogan 'Bolly's is Jolly'. The plastic card on a cord round his neck read 'Circle Security'. The tangle which surrounded the lettering, the Archdeacon, conditioned by his milieu, took to be a crown of thorns. In fact it was a wreath of razor wire.

The rain, which had been threatening all day, had, as the Archdeacon neared the coast, set in in earnest. At eight o'clock on a November Monday evening it was completely dark. The arc lights of Bolly's Jolly Holiday Home were set high above the cluster of buildings. They seemed to vie with the stars for, placed as they were, they cast no light on the ground below them.

The Archdeacon considered whether it might not be like this arriving in limbo after death. After all, we don't really know much from Scripture about that event. It might be more like this than anything else. Except that Archdeacon Treadwell did not much want to enter this particular changed existence. He'd not wanted to come. He'd fought against it. At this time on a Monday evening, after the demands of Sunday, he wanted his own bed, his own fireside, a couple of fingers of Glenmorangie and a nice forty minutes with Inspector Morse. That was the Archdeacon's idea of heaven. He did not pretend to be other than a conventional man.

''S right,' the youth hissed at him. 'They're expecting. Warm Welcome is first left, first right, then first left again past The Kowlabouse. Mind the potholes. They've run out of lamps.'

The Archdeacon edged the car forward over unfamiliar terrain. He feared for his suspension. He did not trust the youth not to have directed him straight over the low cliffs and into the sea, the roar of which he could hear faintly above the hammering of the rain on the car roof and the whining of windscreen wipers. He missed the second turn and ended up facing a tangle of razor wire and a mound of shingle. The rain on the windscreen was tinctured with salt spray and laced with pebbles that clattered on the car like shell shot. What on earth am I doing here, the Archdeacon wondered to himself as he slowly reversed into a pair of dustbins. They were empty and went down like nine pins with a tremendous clattering on the concrete. There they were taken by the wind to roll and joust with each other in a hellish symphony. The Archdeacon wondered whether he should get out and restore them to an upright position if only to stop the row. But noise and water kept him in his seat.

'Warm Welcome' said the corrugated hut in the middle of the tiny square in red flickering neon tubes. The tubes which spelt the 'W' of 'Welcome' had failed so the feeling of the infernal was strengthened. Inside the hut the high command of the diocesan conference team, two very different clerics in the last stages of exhaustion, were crouched either side of a trestle table covered with site plans and timetables. In one corner a huddle of men gazed at notices, their hands cupped round disposable tumblers of a brownish brew. They were not conversing. One or two wore mittens, another a balaclava and greatcoat. There were huge graphs and lists pinned up on the walls, underlined and colour-coded. The feeling here was less of hell than of the HQ of an army in some forgotten outpost. There was a faint smell of wet dog from the steaming coats of the recent arrivals and of fish and chips from those who had been there since lunchtime; screws of greasy paper filled to overflowing the tiny plastic waste-paper basket. A tangle of electric leads to computers, to heaters, to extra lights rendered the floor treacherous to the unwary. A notice twice as high as a house forbade smoking. Another in smaller letters read: 'Welcome to "Millennial Message".' In the corner furthest from the door Canon Oldsalmon puffed his pipe.

At the Archdeacon's entry, the two key men, the conference team organisers, roused themselves from their postures of total exhaustion.

'So you made it.' The Communications Chaplain raised his haggard eyes from his clipboard. He was new in post and quite a lot of people didn't yet recognise him so he'd taken to wearing a big badge on his chest with his photograph in blurry colour on it. Under the photograph was printed 'The Revd Harold Worsted Communications Chaplain'. He had to weigh up whether the comfort that this device gave him was worth the many jokes which it evoked from his colleagues. ('Who are we today, Harold?' 'How's the amnesia?') The title 'Communications Chaplain' had been freshly invented by the new Bishop who called every diocesan administrative officer his chaplain. It seemed to bind them more closely to him personally and cut down any inclinations they might have to strike out on a line of their own or indulge in free thought, which he was against in practice, though for in theory.

Harold did all the work and took the blame. That, he was learning, was what chaplains were for. If there was any success, the Bishop would step in and take the glory. So here he was, tired to death before the conference had even begun, in the middle of his kingdom of notices and wires. He wore fawn cords and a fawn pullover over a black clerical shirt and collar. His hair and complexion were fawn. The Archdeacon thought sometimes that Worsted dressed for camouflage as though he were the final meal in some predator's food chain. But, however much he wished to escape attention, until the Bishop came, Harold was undoubtedly responsible. He was in charge. It was his duty to know.

The last hour had been testing for Harold and his team. Clergy and laity had arrived in small knots at too frequent intervals making outrageous demands like: where do we sleep, where can we eat, where are the bars, has the Bishop arrived? Only the last question could be answered with certainty. 'Not due till tomorrow.'

'One more night in his own bed. Wise man,' the Lay Reader, Ray Cave, had replied to each inquirer. He was a retired bank manager and on that account was supposed to have organising experience. Hence he had been drafted into the 'planning team' for the conference. But, because he was only a layman and the clergy were supposed to be in charge (after all they were the *real* Church), he was never given up-to-date information or told of the many changes of arrangement which would have allowed him to be useful. It was not unlike working for the bank. But then, of course, he'd been paid, now he did it voluntarily.

'Terrible journey. Parts of the diocese I've never seen before,' the Archdeacon admitted.

'No golf courses down Highcliffe on Sea,' agreed Canon Oldsalmon from his (the only comfortable) armchair in the corner. Relaxed, rotund, he was an old campaigner. 'My first living was just round the corner from here. Lowcliffe on Sea. The names reflect the locals' powers of invention. Terrible hole. The only interesting thing that happened in my entire seven years there was the discovery of a set of dinosaur's footprints. The poor beast had staggered there to die.'

Canon Oldsalmon shook out his copy of *The Tablet*. He was adept at making himself at home. Celibate, prayerful, focused on his own particular interpretation of his cure, he could make any temporary resting place his club. Where he was, there comfort would be found.

'Where am I sleeping and where can I eat?' The Archdeacon fixed his eye on the other man at the table. He recognised him as the junior of the team and rightly expected he'd know the domestic arrangements.

'Got the list, Harold?' asked the younger man. He wore no clerical collar, though he was a cleric. He was dressed in the height of youth fashion, his hair shaved to SAS shortness, his trousers of a kind of polished black leather which reflected the light, and a pink T-shirt which said 'Jesus loves me'. He was thirty-four but had worked at being younger than his age for a decade. Chris Teane reckoned the future of the Church lay with youth and he wasn't going to be left behind. He didn't need a label for people to recognise him as 'Youth Chaplain'. He was known everywhere. His forceful beam of goodwill preceded him like a headlight on a dark road, illuminating some but blinding others. He was new in post and reckoned his career under the new Bishop was at last going to take off, not a moment too soon. Gazing at his kit, the Archdeacon was reminded of the boy at the gate. Perhaps it was necessary to dress like them if you were to get on terms with them. Outreach, the Archdeacon thought, in the language of his tribe.

'Give the Archdeacon the pack.' Harold indicated a pile of folders behind him. He felt safe when he said 'the pack'. It looked as though he knew what he was doing and had made some preparations.

'Basic rations. Chalet key, site plan, timetable, guest list, Bishop's welcome letter and worship guide. First left, second right past The Kowlabouse,' said the Youth Chaplain, bestowing the folder on him.

The Archdeacon reckoned he's heard this before. 'I suppose you haven't got a moment to spare to guide me across?'

Chris Teane looked on him pityingly. 'It's not far, it's just across—'

'What number are you?' asked the kind Lay Reader.

The Archdeacon shook the key out of the folder. On one side of its metal tag it said, '247 Happy Holiday Break Block', and, on the other, 'Return to Warm Welcome before you leave. Lost keys will be charged.'

'I'm next door,' said Canon Oldsalmon. 'It's time I had a rest before supper. I'll guide you through the encircling gloom.' He had finished *The Tablet*'s crossword. He heaved himself out of his chair and picked his way nimbly over the electric cables.

Outside the wind had reached gale force. Where the lights cut the blackness rain could be seen slanting on to the glittering, uneven tarmac. Canon Oldsalmon shook out a very large black umbrella and generously offered a half-shoulder span of shelter to the Archdeacon. Together the two elderly men headed into the wind past Kosi Kafé, the Toffy Kounter, the Splendide Diner and Barnees Bowls.

'It all looks a rather temporary sort of building,' the Archdeacon shouted into the wind, gesturing towards the plastic imitations of clapboard and irregular shapes of windows and roof lines.

'Based, I believe, on the Wild West.' Canon Oldsalmon shared his knowledge with his colleague. 'This is Main Street.'

'The what?' The Archdeacon's words were tossed away on the wind.

'The Wild West. Hollywood. The American myth. The idealised past. The innocent and virtuous life of a nation in its formative years. Where men were men, etc.'

'That would explain the spelling,' the Archdeacon hazarded.

Towards the end of the street the ground opened out. There were no more illuminated buildings. The street lamps ceased and, after a moment, when his eyes adjusted, the Archdeacon discerned low blobs of dark against the lighter medium of the sky. The blobs of dark resembled houses in Monopoly. They turned out to be chalets, demountables made of creosoted planks with two doors adjacent to each other giving access to two separate units of accommodation. These were reached from shared steps and a covered overhang which might be called a veranda.

The two priests stumbled up the slippery wooden steps and paused to regroup outside the adjacent doors.

'A snifter?' inquired the Canon.

'Would be very welcome,' the Archdeacon agreed.

There was a fumbling for keys, then a fumbling for a light switch. The rickety door, caught by the wind, flew open. A stale smell of mushrooms and Rentokil met the Archdeacon's nostrils. A room about as big as a billiard table with wooden floor and shallow pitched roof came into view. It was the sort of place where in his youth they had stowed tennis nets and old deckchairs. In Bolly's Jolly Holiday Home they had put in a narrow bunk bed and two wicker chairs. In the corner a red cretonne curtain was drawn back to show a washbasin. It was perishingly cold.

'Bleak,' said the Archdeacon.

'Look on it as a mission field,' suggested his colleague.

'I didn't choose the mission field,' the Archdeacon objected.

'Time to fill a gap in your ministry,' the Canon consoled him.

The Archdeacon would not be comforted. 'I told the Bishop it was madness to have a conference and even greater madness at this time of year and in this place. I'd no idea it was as bad as this.'

'You ain't seen nothing yet,' said the Canon, perhaps affected in his diction by the Wild West decor. 'I understand the Home Office turned it down as temporary overspill accommodation for HM prisons on the grounds of hygiene.'

The Archdeacon shuddered. 'Did you say drink?'

Canon Oldsalmon made for his unpacked bag on his bunk. The bag was of stout impermeable leather which would doubtless keep out the damp. He rummaged for a moment and slipped a silver flask of the type used by race-goers out of the bowels of his baggage and delicately handed it to the Archdeacon first. The warm, sweet, perfumed spirit coursed through the Archdeacon's empty stomach and revived him. He pulled up the other chair quickly and sat down.

'How's Clare?' Canon Oldsalmon had old-fashioned ideas about courtesies to be exchanged before real conversation could begin.

'Probably a good deal more comfortable than I look like being.'

'Many of the laity seem to have brought their wives or, as they call them nowadays, partners, with them.'

The Archdeacon, whose role in the diocese required him to be more up to date than the Canon in his country living, wondered whether it was worth while challenging the view that 'laity' meant the male laity only. He accepted another mouthful of the Canon's whisky and decided it was not. Instead he took up his folder of information and shook out the guest list and programme. His spirits were not raised by the contents.

'I am getting too old to listen to young lay academics telling me what St John's Gospel means.'

'Kenneth Bloomfield from the University of Felixstowe?' hazarded the Canon. The Archdeacon nodded.

'The laicisation of university departments of theology has not extended the Kingdom.' The Canon swilled the whisky round his mouth. It was part of his understanding of the Faith that the world was heading towards Armageddon and there was no point in trying to alter trends that could not be altered. All was in the hand of Providence. This attitude enabled him to bear with equanimity aspects of modern life that the more energetic Archdeacon felt should be challenged.

The Archdeacon turned to the information on worship. Here too he found no comfort. 'The entire thing looks as though it's going to be in the hands of charismatics. Who, in Heaven's name, is Josh the Jester?'

'Ah, now that *is* an interesting invitation.' Canon Oldsalmon had lit a pipe and this made the room seem warmer to the Archdeacon. Or was it the whisky? 'I saw him at the Bishop's consecration. He *is* in orders. He acts the traditional role of the jester in Jacobean drama.' The Canon had read English at Cambridge before turning to test his vocation.

'And that role would be?' The Archdeacon was a theologian pure and simple; some said, unkindly, very simple.

'To mirror back to the world truths it would rather forget. To use nonsense and the *reductio ad absurdum* to show us the error of our ways. He's a spry little fellow and not without the odd insight.'

'And is that going to be the point of this exercise?' The Archdeacon waved his hand in a gesture which took in both the squalor of his surroundings and the conference in general.

'To give us space to reflect on our shortcomings as an institution? Time for amendment of life? Perhaps. Though I think our evangelical brethren see it rather more as a bonding session. Bonding cemented by letting it all hang out, if you'll forgive the mixed metaphors.'

The Archdeacon felt forgiving. Indeed he felt warmer and more relaxed than he had for the past two hours. 'It's odd how Evangelicals have changed. My father and certainly my episcopal grandfather both thought of themselves as Evangelicals but would never have dreamed of letting anything hang out. The were both men of extreme austerity and personal self-discipline. Now Evangelicals are all for bashing cymbals and embracing. It's the Catholic wing which goes in for reason and restraint.' He took another slug of whisky.

'Of course, there are too many voices, too many agendas at dos like this, neither bonding nor self-examination will be accomplished in such conditions.' The Canon drew on his wide ecclesiastical experience.

'Much too noisy. Why *do* we do it?'

'Well, you're supposed to know. Archdeacons are of the inner council. The Bishop's council.'

'It sort of slipped through' – the Archdeacon was apologetic – 'when we weren't looking. And, of course, a new Bishop.'

'With his name to make,' Oldsalmon finished for him. 'And a new Communications Chaplain.'

'With *his* name to make.'

The old men were silent a moment in a shared but unexpressed comment that whatever power it was that had thought that Medwich diocese, which had slumbered quite happily for the past ten years under the same middle-of-the-road bishop, would welcome a Welsh Evangelical, was mistaken.

'I have a feeling of being used.'

'One frequently does in the Church of England. I've noticed. Here we are, sacrificial lambs on the altar of other men's ambitions.'

The Archdeacon remembered his official capacity. He knew he ought to combat this. But the whisky won. 'We are not united,' he agreed. 'Indeed I fear we are mostly at each other's throats.'

'It's lamb.'

'It looks like pork to me.'

'You telling me I don't know my own meat?'

Victor Preserve, manager at Bolly's Jolly Holiday Home, knew his first task was to keep the chef. Replacing a chef in November at short notice in Highcliffe was an impossibility. Two hundred hungry Anglicans wanting fodder every four hours required a chef. Victor knew this. Tibor the chef knew this. It gave Tibor the edge.

'No, I expect you're right,' Victor backed off. 'It's just . . .' Victor smelled the purplish slab in its cover of fawn glue.

'What?'

'It's sort of too thick knit for lamb.'

'Look, what you call it on your menu, that's for you, I don't care. But for my record, it's lamb.' Tibor reckoned he'd won and he wasn't going to argue further. The boil on the back of his neck was aching. He passed his hand over it and winced.

Victor, a properly trained student of Catering Studies at Felixstowe Poly (now University), wondered if he should tell Tibor to wash his hands after he'd done that. Then he thought of the replacement problem and refrained.

Victor drew breath, which wasn't easy in the fumy atmosphere of the kitchen and against the noise of two tough Italian ladies and an old, old Irishman preparing two hundred dinners on a plant designed for a hundred and fifty and on a budget screwed down to the last penny every Monday morning by a slab-faced accountant who looked as though he lived on water and sandpaper.

'You're all right then?' Victor asked. 'You can cope OK?'

'Don't I look all right?' The large cook suddenly looked worried.

That's more like it. That's the Tibor I know and hate, Victor thought, the hypochondriac with every reason to fear for his health. But it was Victor's only way of keeping him in order. He'd be safe to leave now. 'See you for breakfast. Right? You won't be late? I don't want to have to do it myself.'

'Get out.' Tibor's hand went to his neck.

'You ought to—' Victor began.

'What?' The big chef swung round on the smaller manager.

'Nothing. See you.'

'It's a good thing we brought the lamp. I like a good light to see my book by.'

Lucy Royal smiled at Arthur Royal and carefully they placed their identical canvas bags on the twin bunks of number 250 Happy Holiday Break Block. The window ran with condensation. They knew better than to unpack. Indeed there was nothing to unpack into. Instead, as two dancers in the same well-rehearsed ballet, they took out sleeping bags and pullovers. That done, Arthur produced a small camping-gaz stove and Lucy extracted a tiny kettle, just big enough for a large mug of tea each.

Arthur bent his fine-boned face with the remains of a tropical tan, now converted into freckles and blotches, towards his plump wife. He was eighty-two, she eighty-one. Together they had half a century's experience in the mission field of West Africa, he a doctor, she a nurse. There was nothing they did not know about survival of all sorts, physical first, but also psychological, moral and spiritual. They had surmounted all sorts of obstacles and worked, sometimes even successfully, in hostile climates, under brutal regimes, in the face of horrendous diseases, sometimes in isolation, sometimes in overcrowding. They had met and together triumphed. They had rarely been parted. They had supported each other and cared for large numbers of others, helping to alleviate the many sorts of suffering caused by men and the rather smaller number caused by nature.

'Isn't it lovely to be here?' Lucy smiled her rosy smile and plumped up their sleeping bags. She placed her Bible and Book of Common Prayer on the table on her side of the bed. 'We mustn't make ourselves so cosy here that we forget our mission, must we? But I can see it's going to be such fun.' She handed Arthur his steaming mug. 'Now read me the Bishop's letter and then we can have a little nap before supper.'

They divided the chores of life between them according to the reliability of their faculties. Arthur's eyes were better than Lucy's, her hearing more acute than his. Hence he shook the Bishop's letter from the information pack, found the right bit of his bi-focals, cleared his throat and began. 'Brothers and sisters in Christ, as you know, in the early Church . . .' Unconsciously Arthur's Cambridge tones modified into the Welsh lilt of the Bishop. Lucy giggled. Outside the wind roared as it drove the tide on to the shifting sands. The sounds of nature mingled, could it be, with a murmur of voices from next door? Was she dozing, she wondered, or were there really people talking near at hand?

The voices were low but distinct. Were both men's or was one of them a woman with a low register? The hubbub of the wind made it difficult to say. Doors slammed, shutters rattled and polythene slapped but above or perhaps below the noise she could definitely make out a conversation.

'Of course he's ambitious. Aren't they all?'

'They being?'

'The Welsh.'

'The senior clergy.'

'I haven't known many.'

'One is enough.'

'Bishop Jonah Emery, straight out of Pontypridd via Lampeter.'

'Not perhaps the most tactful choice for a rural English diocese.'

'He doesn't know his men.'

'Women.'

'Women don't count.'

'He doesn't walk the floor.'

'He wouldn't dare.'

'If he did, someone would put a knife between his shoulders.'

'Love from Forward in Faith.'

'Even the Evangelicals find him difficult.'

'They think they can use him.'

'He's too maverick to be used.'

'So what's going to happen?'

'We don't need to lift a finger. With Worsted in charge nothing is going to work.'

'Lighting and sound systems.'

'Room designations and direction notices.'

'Food and drink.'

'Worship?'

'They'll all cut their own throats there without any help from us.'

'Trying to construct rituals which have no roots in life.'

'Casting seaweed into the sea.'

'Meaningless.'

'Worse. Embarrassing.'

'It's going to be a really jolly do.'

CHAPTER TWO

Highcliffe on Sea

'Ignorance shared is ignorance excused, I always say.'

Theodora Braithwaite, a woman in her thirties in deacon's orders in the Church of England, thought she knew that voice. Her instinct was to hide but the train was crowded. She might not find another seat or even (she eyed the tangle of legs, bodies and arms which cluttered the carriage) be able to get out of her present one.

'I suppose we all tend to feel . . .' The answering voice was hesitant, deferential, the voice of a younger man.

Theodora was surprised at how clearly she could hear both voices given the noise of the train and the number of people in the carriage. She supposed that years of making yourself heard in cathedrals with dampening acoustics and halls with inadequate sound systems had sharpened the skills of at least the older man. She was nearly sure it was . . . She risked glancing round quickly. Yes, it was Bishop Jonah Emery, Dundrearies bristling from his cheeks like an ageing fox terrier, little grey eyes snapping above the mouth which seemed to be constantly in motion, even on the rare occasion when he was not speaking. 'Always chewing his next enemy', an ill-wisher had once said of him.

Theodora thought how little she wanted to have to listen to him. Why wasn't he in his chauffeur-driven Rover instead of clarting up the public transport system? Those who had a right to private cars ought to use them. Theodora, raised amidst the clerical hierarchy, a daughter of eight generations of Anglican priests, did not at all grudge the senior clergy their privileges. What she did deprecate was the inverted snobbery, the inconvenient false humility of denial. On the other hand, she caught herself up, probably a six a.m. start, the lack of a restaurant car and the thought of five days' physical and social discomfort might have curdled her spirits.

The Bishop must be bound for the Highcliffe conference. It was enough to make one turn back right now. She viewed the future with gloom. The only reason she had been lured to forsake her beloved parish of Betterhouse on the south bank of the Thames in west London, was an invitation to speak on 'The Diaconate and the Women's Question'. The invitation had come from Father Raymond Sentinel. She recalled his letter of invitation, written in his small spiky hand in black ink on very thick creamy paper rather foxed at the edges. The address at the top had been engraved before the latest telephone codes. It said Wrackheath 236, which, when she had rung to confirm her acceptance, had confused the operator.

She conjured up the figure of Father Raymond. He must now, surely, be well into his eighties. She remembered his skin, so pale as to be almost transparent, stretched over his skull-like head with a thin coating of silver hair presaging the heavenly region whither doubtless he would be transported in the not too distant future. He was a walking *memento mori. She* had accepted because he was an old friend of her family. Her dead father in his north Oxford parish had looked upon him as a spiritual mentor; her great-uncle, Canon Hugh Braithwaite, late of Ely, had been his contemporary at Oxford. *He* had invited her because he knew he could trust her. 'The title of your paper,' he had written, 'is, as you may imagine, not of my own choosing. A more becoming phraseology might be "The Diaconate and Women's Ministry". However, our new Bishop looks at these matters from the other end of the telescope. I do hope your duties will allow you to help us out if Father Geoffrey can spare you for a few days. I am not sure that I can promise you congenial company but there will be a few of the faithful to keep the cause going. A remnant, at least.' By this he meant those who were opposed to women in priests' orders. Theodora had come to feel that women seeking to be priested were too often led by the desire for political and positional power. And indeed, who, at one level, should blame them? For generations they had manned the tea urns and watched the chaps taking the lead. This could cut both ways. Sometimes the domestic chores *were* what the women were best at, but sometimes, from the point of view of sheer worldly efficiency, they would have done better to swap places. For her own part, however, Theodora had resolved that she would not be priested but continue as deacon. She found it better not to get involved in arguments about it because it was difficult to articulate her reasons and sounded masochistic. Nevertheless, she felt herself to be on sure ground in arguing that spiritual power is quite different from political or social power and that clergy should not be concerned at all with the latter but only the former. If Father Raymond had not been a family friend, she would not have accepted. As it was she had come to feel it was time someone tried to put the difficult case that they should let the chaps get on with running the world if they wanted but that it was for the women to keep alive the notion of the spiritual life. Listening, as she now had no choice but to do, to Bishop Jonah, she all but repented of her decision.

'My meaning is this,' the Bishop was continuing. (Theodora caught the Welsh lilt in his voice and the didactic tone. Was he wagging his finger as she had seen him do?) 'If we find other people share our ignorance, we feel we don't have to remedy it. It affirms us in our lack of understanding. Ignorance is contagious. And it's no different in the Church. We look round our fellow clergy and what do we see?'

There was a pause and Theodora imagined the Bishop looking round. 'We see we are all ignorant. We do not understand what the world wants from us. That's why we are here today. No. Cross that out. For these precious few days. We're here to find out what people want from us. If we don't find out soon . . .' The Bishop trailed off. Theodora thought he might end 'they won't vote for us'. Instead he continued, 'And that's where the Church comes in. If the man and woman in the street don't understand us, we'll just have to change our tune until we find one we can all sing together.'

Theodora thought that that was a very good summary of what was wrong with the upper echelons of the Church of England. It was rumoured that the Bishop did not want *particular* changes in the Church, just changes. If it existed, change it, was his motto. Liturgy, the parish system, clergy training, establishment, what he called 'plant' and by that meant parish churches older than a decade, were all so much baggage as far as he was concerned. Phrases like 'on task' and 'on message' surrounded him as gnats on a horse in summer. He had made his way not by reason and analysis but by using the catchphrases of the moment. All was justified by 'relevant', 'Millennium' and 'youth'. He fitted easily on to the current bench of Bishops.

She heard what she took to be the younger man acting out his role of audience. This was not a conversation, she realised, but a rehearsal, probably for the Bishop's opening-of-conference speech.

'Our little time together here, in this pleasant seaside spot, will give us a respite, a welcome breathing space (Paul, 1 Corinthians) to take stock of our shared ignorance and to vigorously . . . vigorously to remedy it.'

This was undoubtedly the peroration of his address. She waited for the applause. The other man (could it be the Reverend Russell Peach, the Bishop's chaplain?) seemed to feel that something was due as well. He could be heard murmuring ardently to fill the gap. 'Really inspiring . . . valuable exercise . . . welcome opportunity.'

Theodora recalled Peach's curly golden hair and reckoned there were positions in the Church's hierarchy even lower than her own. At least she did not have to flatter the tenth-rate. Her own place as curate to a sane and hardworking inner city priest, Geoffrey Brighouse, gave her scope for talent and harmony in her relationships. At least I have the illusion of being useful, she thought. And then thought of what she would have to say at Highcliffe. How could she make her argument truthful and clear, without sounding pretentious or sanctimonious? The majority of people at the conference, both men and women, clerical and lay, would be against her position. Most priests, most people were temperamentally incapable of seeing the difference between political power and spiritual power and no amount of quotation from Scripture altered them. The men were in love with it, the women wanted a share of it. She might as well catch the next train back to Betterhouse.

She glanced out of the window. They were even now travelling though the low-lying back lands of Highcliffe. Here marshes filled surreptitiously with salt water when the tide flooded, canals with sluggish flow impeded more than they enhanced drainage. A few greyish sheep raised their faces infrequently from their main task of gathering a living from the ungenerous fields.

She had been here as a child and adolescent on one of

her many East Anglian holidays. Like all the east coast resorts it was cold and windswept with a grey sea breaking on weed-encrusted, rotting breakwaters. You wore pullovers on the beach in August and bathed only if family pressures forced you. Because it was uncomfortable it was assumed, in the dour ethic of East Anglia, to be healthy, especially for children. They came with their nannies and au pairs while the sensible parents flew to Greece.

She remembered the place in her teens. Had it perhaps been on her last holiday there before the freedom of university life had put an end to the pretence of family holidays? She had thought to herself that Highcliffe on Sea always seemed either too empty or, for about two months in the summer, too full. Sand infiltrated places where it should not, an insidious presage of decay. The sea spray and air were pungent, especially destructive of paint. Every year windowsills and gable boards needed to be scraped free of the tough furl of curling paint and repainted. Indeed, painting was one of the few local industries that prospered. Things were either painted, in which case it was the season, or they were in need of repainting, in which case it was out of season.

When the Medwich diocesan conference was held in Bolly's Jolly Holiday Home it was out of season. Indeed it was out of season by a couple of months. And for that reason, Theodora surmised, cheap. She could remember roughly where the camp was but hadn't ever actually set foot in it. It had been surrounded with barbed-wire entanglements which looked as though they had been left over from the Second World War, though whether to keep the natives out or the guests in, was unclear. She'd never stayed in a holiday camp. She looked forward to extending her experience.

As the train rounded into the straight she pressed her face against the glass and looked back at the higher ground which encircled the resort to the west. There it was, the trees and chalk workings of Wrackheath. Theodora turned her mind from the place. To be sure it was another reason for accepting the invitation but it was not one she cared to think about. She'd promised to visit, but not until after the conference. One set of problems at a time.

'What I want to know' – the tone was belligerent – 'is why when the programme says the Bishop isn't due till lunch today and the official opening isn't until this afternoon's session, why, I say, did they get us down here for last night?'

Daniel Ripe liked a good blame. It was almost the only pleasure left to him in life. He had a difficult parish, he'd been in it far too long, nobody ever told him how brave he was or how difficult his furrow was to plough. Nobody knew the troubles he had. He'd compensated by honing a technique of splashing blame around like lighter fuel. What he wanted, wanted all the time, was a damn good row. It was frustrating that he had chosen a profession the majority of whose members were dedicated to turning other cheeks; the general emollience of his colleagues often drove him to shrieking point. Other times he just wanted to cry. Today he'd had a miserable breakfast of pre-sweetened corn flakes and a rusty-looking sausage. He was all geared up for a run in with someone, anyone, before the first session. So he trundled along to the Warm Welcome office. He put a little case down by his feet, stood protectively over it, leaned across the trestle table and prepared for battle.

Chris Teane looked at him with contempt. He belonged, temperamentally at least, to a younger generation of clergy who didn't see what Daniel was on about. If he didn't like his lot he should either change it or shut up. His was not a mind that could realise how absolutely essential it was to Daniel's sanity that he should be allowed to whinge.

'And I'll tell you another thing,' Daniel was getting under

way, 'I haven't got a map in my pack either. And another thing . . .' The more Daniel scented an unsympathetic ear the closer he reckoned to engage. At last it looked as though he might get a rise. 'And another thing. All last night there was a door banging approximately every six and a half minutes. I couldn't get a wink.' He stopped in triumph and to get his breath. His long lugubrious face seemed out of scale with his short body and legs. But the impact was powerful all the same. Harold Worsted was visibly cringing.

Daniel turned from the unyielding Teane to the more sympathetic ear of Ray Cave. 'I bet you lot have got yourselves decent quarters. Yes?'

'Well, actually,' Ray said, 'I don't think there are any decent quarters. Not as such.' His years as a bank manager had inured him to whingers. 'I mean, they're all draughty, a bit damp and cramped.'

'So where are you putting the Bishop?' Daniel was triumphant.

'In the flat above Harries Bar. They haven't got a resident barman at the moment so it was vacant if a bit smelly. Beer and tobacco fumes seem to waft up from below but it's warmer than the chalets.'

'Going to take his turn pulling the pints, is he? I doubt it.' Daniel liked to set up an unlikely scenario and then blame someone for its not being realised. He'd found it an effective ploy for winding up his adversaries. It left people baffled.

Daniel seemed to think he'd won some sort of round. He was almost jolly. 'Well now, where can I do my washing?'

'What?'

'Washing. You know, shirts and pants. Put them in hot water to get them clean?'

'Why on earth do you want to do your washing here?' Ray was caught off guard. As a bank manager, he'd been immaculately turned out; for forty years clean shirt and socks were his daily lot. When she had been alive his dear wife had done him proud. Since her death he'd carried on the noble tradition. He'd learned in the sea cadets in his youth and laundered his own. He enjoyed the task. There had been no break. He gazed at Daniel's crumpled black shirt and red knitted tie located at some distance from a buttonless collar. Daniel, at Westcott in the sixties, had admired Alec Vidler. Ray hesitated to speculate on his underclothes.

'Since her last breakdown, Cherry hasn't been able to wash. She's got an allergy to the powder. And anyway, the machine's playing up. It flooded the kitchen Sunday night. So I've brought a load to do here. So where is it?'

'I know.' Harold Worsted was naturally proud of this. He didn't get much right in the organisational life. 'The laundrette's in Shane Lane.' He pushed the site map across the table. 'Next to the RCs' chapel on the other side of the massage parlour.'

Chris Teane sniggered.

'The chapel used to be a sweet shop.' Worsted risked looking disapprovingly at Teane. 'It's a recent conversion.'

Teane grinned again. 'Not a cradle Catholic.'

'Righty ho,' said Daniel hitching his crumpled trousers up and making for the door.

His exit coincided with Bishop Emery's entrance. Bishops do not move around on their own. They gather to themselves a posse of acolytes, an entourage. A lesser man than Daniel would have stood aside. But to Daniel they merely presented a challenge. He began to thread his way through the train until he reached the Bishop in person.

'Morning, Chris.' The Bishop prided himself on having learned his clergy's names, anyway their first names, very fast. Christopher, Stephen, Bryan and Michael were his favourite ones. And since these *were* the names of the majority of the clergy in their forties and fifties, he was on average quite likely to be right.

'Hi, Jonah,' replied Daniel, to show that all were equal in the brotherhood of Christ.

The Bishop, who thought this too in theory but didn't like it in practice, pushed towards the desk amidst a general rising and scraping of chairs.

'Daniel,' said Daniel.

The Bishop did not look back. There was a chorus of 'Good morning, Bishop, safe journey then. Have you breakfasted?'

'There are just one or two things I need to check out with—' Worsted began.

'Yes, yes, yes,' said the Bishop. 'First session ten o'clock. Taking stock of the Millennium. We need to get our skids on. I want that first meeting to be a real hands-on, coats-off session. Work groups,' he threatened. 'A really honest look at ourselves. Where is our ministry going? Eh?' He looked round. A number of clergy and one or two laymen who had crowded into the suddenly small office felt it safe to nod.

'Would you like a' – Worsted offered the folder – 'pack?' He held it as though putting a titbit through the bars of a lion's cage. The Bishop waved it away. His chaplain scooped it up.

Theodora had prudently waited until the Bishop and his chaplain had gathered themselves together and left the train. The Bishop carried a slim black leather document case; his chaplain a large tartan holdall and a small green canvas one. He had walked behind Bishop Emery. The Bishop was short and spry, the chaplain was tall and gangling. They looked like a comedy duo. Perhaps this is what the Church of England has come to, an entertainment with visual jokes, Theodora reflected.

The chaplain had secured the last taxi in the rank. Theodora thought of the breakfast she had not had time to wait for after serving for her vicar at early mass. She smelled bacon and followed the trail. 'Laddy's Café', it said, 'Breakfast All Day.' A better bet, Theodora reckoned, than a three-mile trek across town to a tepid cup of khaki-coloured liquid, which would likely be the conference-goers lot. The tide which could be heard in the distance was bringing rain with it. She would be a bit late clocking in, but then she'd heard the Bishop's opening address. Laddy's curtainless windows ran with condensation. The vapour from the urn looked like a print of an early steam engine.

The chef's speciality was dripping toast. Theodora took her plate and mug of sweet strong Indian tea to the corner furthest from the door and prepared to complete *The Times'* crossword. Only gradually did she become aware of the conversation to her left.

'You can't eat it,' said the first, a man' voice. There was a pause. The tone suggested there was no argument with this.

'Oh, we're talking luxury here, I grant you.' The younger voice, also male, answered. The tone was judicious. Theodora's habit of trying to fix context to words was defeated here. For a start, the voices didn't fit the place. The older man's voice was old fashioned. He could command all the vowels which the English language requires. The younger had the same timbre but was fashionably glottal. 'T's were omitted and vowels flattened to produce the nasal twang of the new English ubiquitous amongst the young, both educated and uneducated, as though he might know different but couldn't be bothered. Or was it, Theodora speculated, that he feared that if he spoke as the older man did, he might be cut off from the crowd or from his own, younger world. She pondered on the two disparate tones which seemed to her to characterise a whole social upheaval, bloodless, without bitterness or violence, to be sure, but which cut the generations in half. Either you spoke old English or you spoke new English; the speech rhythms, the syntax and vocabulary were quite different from each other. She thought of her own Cheltenham tones formed twenty-five years ago. On the cusp, she wondered, or just in under the net? Her own tone, in her many-toned parish, with its community of Chinese, Turks, Cypriots, Indians and Pakistanis, did not set her apart. She was accepted as just one more in the pot. Hers was not the accent of the ascendancy, for the Church in St Sylvester's Betterhouse was as poor and struggling as the rest. That was why she liked it and why she stayed.

'But if you *did*, you know, put it back how it was . . .' The younger man's tone was cajoling, explorative.

'How it was when? In your Uncle Timothy's time? In your great-grandfather's? In the baronet's? Your problem is you don't know any history. I mean, where would you stop?'

'I'm surprised at you, Dad. You're supposed to be the traditionalist, preserving old times. I'm supposed to be the young Turk, all for change and that.'

Theodora went to work again. She had the impression of a very young man pretending, claiming a more mature role than he might feel he could live up to, but sincere for all that, not disingenuous.

'You've still got to pay the bills. Beauty can't do that.' This had not the same sincerity, more an adoption of a posture. It was a move it would be reasonable to take but which in fact the older man did not believe in. Neither beauty nor bills really moved him. He wasn't *engaged* in this discussion.

'But if it's something to revive us, cheer everyone up . . .' The young man was urgent now, pleading almost.

'It wouldn't.' The older man left his posturing. He was incisive. 'It only fits certain tastes. *You* like it, but it excludes as many as it delights.'

'But—' The young man sought to get back again. The older talked him down.

'And anyway, you haven't got the wherewithal. So it's all a chimera.'

'I might have. I told you.'

'That's hogwash, old boy. You couldn't go down that road. It ended in disaster last time. Keep away from what you can't handle.'

Theodora felt rather than heard the mutinous look on the boy's face. She turned her head and peered over *The Times*. Then she ducked back again. Why hadn't she recognised the voices? Probably because it was ten years since she had heard either of them. But that was undoubtedly them. Both of them. How extraordinary to see them both in the steam and frying fat of Laddy's.

Her cousin, Randolph, she recognised now, remembering the thick grey hair which looked as though he cut it himself with a razor. His son, Nicholas, who had been perhaps eleven when she last saw him, she would not have recognised. He'd grown tall in prison and a diffident manner had become a sort of querulous persistence which she'd seen in other youngsters in her prison-visiting. They didn't have courage but a kind of survivor's tenacity which stood them in good stead. The din in Laddy's was beginning to subside. The breakfast rush had gone. There'd be a gap before the lunch trade came in. Theodora wondered if she should make herself known. After all, she'd come to Highcliffe with more than just the conference in view.

She peered again at the pair. Cousin Randolph wore a brown corded velvet jacket well past its first youth and a pair of grey pin-striped trousers which had belonged to a suit. His son had the usual grey chinos of youth and a thin blue nylon anorak of the camping equipment kind with pockets in surprising places. The pair of them looked seedy but not furtive or subdued as she might have supposed, given their fortune, but rather jaunty and undaunted. They also looked related; no one would have supposed that they were other than father and son. Only, Theodora thought, they might have concluded at moments that Nick was the father and Randolph his son.

Randolph put his head back to drain the dregs of his tea. He patted his son on the arm. 'No point in killing ourselves with worry. Your mother wouldn't have wanted that.'

'Dad, I'd like to see it right—'

'Too far gone for that, old boy.'

'If it comes off . . .'

'My advice would be let it alone. You're not cut out for that sort of thing.' There was no urgency or disapproval in his tone, just a statement of an oft spoken and mutually recognised fact. They'd been here before.

They rose together. Theodora raised *The Times* a fraction. She lacked the courage to encounter the pair of them as they made their way into the street. They had seemed so close, it would have been an intrusion to present herself. She watched the street door swing to behind them. There was no longer any excuse. Bolly's Jolly Holiday Home called her now.

The conference was in full swing by ten-thirty. There'd been one or two hiccups in getting everyone to the same, right place; some of the sign-posting had gone a bit awry. But this was only to be expected in an unfamiliar venue at the start of proceedings. 'Teething troubles', a lot of people had remarked to each other. Anglicans like to forgive someone. The hall of The Kowlabouse was packed. For the four months of summer it was crammed. In the evening there would be a continuous disco, in the morning bingo 'for the wrinklies', as the manager before Victor had put it. But the place had never seen anything like the present audience. The bar at the back was closed but the smell of beer and Virginia tobacco clung to the heavy velvet curtains. Otherwise, Victor thought, looking in from the kitchen after a quick wrestle with Tibor, everything so far appeared to be on target.

A holiday camp manager's life is meant to be one crisis after another and so it was. But some crises are bigger than others. Tibor had got in on time to do the breakfast. But there were more conference-goers wanting breakfast than the diocesan team had given him to expect. The client was always right, of course, his polytechnic catering course training had told him, but having had his daily meeting with Harold Worsted he had rather wondered. Now, as he surveyed the ranks of clergy and laity, he felt it would be all right. He had a nose for a conference. He'd been at it eighteen months now, two summers. Career-wise, as he put it to himself, he ought to have moved on, but curiosity had stayed him. He knew nothing of the Church. Who were they and what would they do? So far in conference terms he'd managed hang gliders, Jewish vegetarians (a right pain they'd been for Tibor; they'd brought their own cook and the fighting had been continuous) and the association of lawn-mower sales personnel. The latter were rather his level. His ambition was Rotarians but they wanted better food than Bolly's could offer and the accommodation was not up to their scratch either. Still, he lived in hope, and the clergy were surely a notch up the scale. Some day, he dreamed, he'd be catering for conferences of Japanese in Birmingham. The sky, quite frankly, was the limit. He'd told Sharon just before she'd left him. He was going to make it. But she'd gone off with a man whose dad had his own boat yard outside Felixstowe and could make his own hours. Ever fair minded, Victor could see he was a better bet prospects wise. Still, for the moment, everything was going fine, just fine.

Theodora paused in the doorway and snuffed the scent

of her co-workers in Christ. The conference-goers had begun to thaw and bond. New members of the clergy were being introduced to the diocese. The Reverend Martin Guard (thin white clerical collar, neat black suit proclaiming his Anglo-Catholic allegiance) stood to relaxed attention and explained he'd been a naval gunnery officer before taking orders. Now he was looking forward to (he implied) making a success of the parish of St Lawrence, Wrackheath. Father Sentinel, siting beside him, bonily clapped his hands together. He was applauded more warmly than his churchmanship and his evident and therefore threatening efficiency would normally have evoked. Why? Theodora wondered. Perhaps people had to let off some energy. There was much goodwill. Next, by way of contrast, a flabby-looking man with a green pullover and no outward sign of his priestly calling admitted he was forty-four and had previously 'been in oil'. He paused, blushed and added he was to be married next month. More applause and laughter. An athletic-looking African then rose and agreed he'd entered the diocese with some trepidation because he'd heard English Christians were cold, 'well, cooler,' than he'd been used to in Zimbabwe, But he had to say he hadn't found anything to complain about in the warmth of his welcome. Hallelujah! the Evangelicals echoed him.

Theodora slipped into the end of a row of plastic stackables thoughtfully put out for late-comers. A row or two ahead she recognised a familiar pair of laity. Dr and Mrs Royal, if she mistook her not. Her spirits lifted. She'd try and have a word at the coffee break. On the front row she glimpsed Archdeacon Treadwell. He'd aged since she last met him, dear man. Constantly facing the challenges of a changing Church had taken it out of him. Further down, near Raymond Sentinel, was a face she found familiar but couldn't immediately put a name to. Could it be, yes it was, Canon Oldsalmon. She'd known him when she was an undergraduate and he'd preached regularly at Pusey House. Not all that changed.

Now it was the turn of the Bishop's address. Theodora prepared to hear again the words rehearsed on the train. The Bishop darted up on to the platform followed by his faithful chaplain. They both carried what the more naïve of the laity took to be Bibles but which were in fact Filofaxes. The Bishop seized the microphone as though it were intent on getting away from him.

'Fellow workers in the Kingdom,' he began, 'I want to use our precious time together over the next few days to take a long hard look at ourselves, to see where we are, how stand we and then, under the guidance of the Holy Spirit, to think where we should be.' He'd learned these unexceptional phrases at a marketing conference for senior clergy at St George's, Windsor. He steadied the microphone in his left hand and made a gesture like a conductor with his right. The overhead projector jumped into life and the screen high above the little Bishop's head was illuminated. He snapped his fingers and the first picture sprang up. There was a slight intake of breath, an uncertain giggle or two and then uneasy silence. The Bishop, certain of his ground, tapped his script. 'This is where we are,' he said sternly.

His audience gazed at a coloured slide of an opulent bed on which a lady and a gentleman were showing more than mere affection for each other. The chaplain could be heard coughing heavily and attempting to attract his master's attention. The Bishop was not to be diverted.

'I repeat,' the Bishop pressed on, 'this is where we are. But it's not good enough. Figures can't lie. We need' – he paused and leaned forward – 'we need to be much more self-aware and do a lot better than this. We have nothing to be ashamed of, have we? Paul, Romans—'

The Reverend Russell Peach felt this had gone on long enough. He scraped back his chair and hurried towards the Bishop. The Bishop swung round, still holding the microphone, as though to fend him off. Peach stopped in his tracks and gestured towards the screen behind them.

'Bishop, I don't think . . .'

'What?'

'Your slides are, er, out of order.'

The Bishop swung round and gazed at the image behind him. A look of bafflement spread over his features. 'What's going on?'

'Mixed slides?'

'You did?'

'No, no. Not me. I haven't touched them. I thought perhaps you?'

'Don't be idiotic, Peach, what would I want with this? Not of course that there is anything wrong with or indeed distasteful about the sexual act.' He stared at the subdued audience, quelling their prurience with a headmasterly frown and then looked back at the image. 'But it isn't relevant to what I want to say. I want a pie chart of church attendance figures in the diocese over the last decade. You'd better see if you can find it.' He indicated the carousel.

Peach moved reluctantly towards the apparatus and hesitated. Theodora inferred that audio-visuals were not his thing. Havering for a moment, Peach then began to rotate the carousel gingerly. It was apparent that in between pie charts of Church attendance figures, and jolly-looking Christians blamelessly involved in playing with scout troops and baptisms, had been interposed shots which were not concerned specifically with Church matters. Peach swung unhappily round. 'I'll have to re-sort.'

The Bishop snorted. 'I'll do without. The devil shall not triumph.'

Peach switched off the light of the OHP. The room settled down with murmurs of subdued conversation. Theodora found the spectacle interesting. What had happened? It wasn't clear at the back, at first, whether the Bishop had meant to put on a show with some sort of shock in it or whether it was a joke or a mistake. Theodora could see Lucy Royal a row or two in front composedly passing a boiled sweet to Arthur as though to a fractious child in an over-long service.

The Bishop, only slightly ruffled, got into his stride again. The words, familiar to Theodora, began to flow from him. She had to admit he had charisma. The slightly sung delivery, the passion and sincerity began to penetrate his audience. After all, perhaps everything would go well. The mood was tolerant, even high. The clergy liked to feel they were amongst their own kind and even lay Christians were cheered to see some new members instead of the same old faces. The Bishop came to his peroration. Theodora's mind wandered to her own problems. She thought of the paper she herself would, in time, at the end of the conference, have to deliver. She noticed at the far side by the main exit the young man who had been in the Warm Welcome when she'd arrived, and remembered his badge said 'Manager' over his black and white T-shirt with 'Bolly's is Jolly' on it. She saw him turn to a younger man with short cropped orange hair and an earring also dressed in the Bollys' uniform. Then she saw him dash out of the back door. A crisis with lunch perhaps. She returned her attention to the Bishop. Who, she wondered, had muddled the slides? And to what end? He clearly wasn't a man to be distracted from his tasks by any little mishap. But, she speculated, from the muddle over the slides, Bishop Emery might just find his powers being tested to the full.

Victor looked at the Reverend Daniel Ripe and said in his best managers-are-not-fazed-by-anything voice, 'You're sure it was a *dead* body?'

'I've seen enough,' said Daniel, 'and actually, though I've

never told anyone this, I once gave the last rites to one. The wife was keen and I didn't like to let on the husband was dead. So, yes, I'd say it was dead.'

'And where exactly did you say it was you found it?'

'I told your colleague here.' Daniel indicated the red-haired boy. 'In the washing machine. I'd just put my stuff in one of those plastic basket thingys when I saw this leg poking out. To be honest I didn't see it *as* a leg, if you know what I mean. If you're not expecting something you try and make sense of it in terms you are expecting. I wasn't expecting bodies but I was prepared for clothes, you see. So I thought, Hello, that's a trouser with a sock on it. It took me a minute to realise . . .' He trailed off. Naturally prolix, the fact of death did in the end subdue him.

'We'd better clear this one up,' Victor said as though it might be an unfortunate spillage somewhere. He frankly didn't find Daniel all that convincing. There was something off centre about him. Victor led the way out of the Warm Welcome office and walked, not running (no Bolly's Staff Officer ever runs) towards the street parallel to Main Street called Wayne Lane, past the Blazing Saddles Card, Sweet and Tobacco shop along to the massage parlour and the launderette.

The three of them pulled up at the door which Daniel had left open. The room smelt of old socks and washing powder. The four machines stood on one side of the space and four tumble-dryers on the other. Various dispensers of powders were fitted on to the walls. When it had been equipped laundrettes had been in an early stage of development. It had not been painted or cleaned for some time. Daniel stood at the door and indicated the machine at the end of the row. Gingerly Victor approached and bent down.

CHAPTER THREE

Wrackheath

Very carefully Nick pushed the rubberised sealant into the crack and prodded at it with a screwdriver. The instructions on the tin advised that the two ingredients therein should be mixed thoroughly according to a quantitative formula. But Nick wasn't too good at figures and quantities. They'd changed over to metrics when he was halfway through his schooling and he'd not really caught on to either system. So he guessed. It also said the surface should be dry and clean before applying. He looked at the long fungus-filled crack in the cement running down the side and into the middle of the tank. His hands were cold and the rain, which came into Highcliffe this time of year with every tide, rendered the air dank inside the stone basin in the garden at Wrackheath.

The tank was part of what had once been Wrackheath's formal gardens in the time of the seventh baronet, Nick's Edwardian Great-uncle Matthew. Sir Matthew had left his mark on the place. The gardens had been done over especially to entertain the Prince of Wales, in formal terraced parterres ending in pergolas, shrubberies and woodland sloping down to the main road into Highcliffe. Now only the outline of the planting of the great-uncle could be seen by the eye of faith. Lawns merged into gravelled paths with scarcely a hesitation; beds were marked only by a change in level. The stone bowls of the jardinières were pitted with dark lichen. They reared up and stood, chipped and empty, dotted in no discernible pattern over the terrace. One way and another Uncle Matthew had done for the family fortune never very soundly established. He'd spent and speculated, gambled and crashed in the way of highest fashion of the time. The Prince of Wales had not, in fact, in the end accepted the invitation.

Nick gave one last poke at the rubberised solution and then clambered out of the tank. It wasn't, he could see, going to work. Nothing worked here. Nothing that he did was any good. The decay was just too vast. Year in and year out, day by day, nature had encroached. He remembered how, as a child, he'd been happy to play amidst the decay. In a way it was a child's paradise. The conservatory sported growths never dreamt of in the days of gardeners. The overgrown shrubbery was a tangle for the imagination to roam in. He'd ridden an old pony down the rides before they'd sold off the timber and the brambles had closed in.

But with adolescence and young manhood Nick had become aware that buildings are more than just dreamlands to fantasise and play in. That the house had presence, he had always known. But gradually he began to perceive it as having a more profound and personal worth. It was not just that he recognised that as a building it had a place in history and a significance in the geography of the local landscape. It was rather that it had a numinous quality that sometimes he called beauty. He remembered the first time when this had dawned on him. He'd been brought back from one of his frequent but brief stays at a boarding school. The car had turned the bend and he'd seen the house as though for the first time. It had been November then too, the trees were bare, leaves piled in the ruts of the drive. Water had begun to seep through the stucco to leave dark maps on the façade. He'd realised then that a house which has a history, which has, like a person, celebrated and suffered, is worthy of respect. It was greater than he but it also needed him.

Sir Darius Trimming had picked the spot on the hills behind Highcliffe in 1790 because he could race his horses from there to Ipswich along a roughly straight road in under the hour. He'd wanted something solid and handsome to counter the flimsiness of his life and fortune but also something curious and ingenious to work the imaginations and evoke the envy of his Hell-fire Club cronies. He designed the exterior himself and brought in a pupil of Soane to do the inside. The result was in all the histories of architecture. A pediment and three-bay portico with slender double Doric columns and a curved double staircase ensured its place in Pevsner, whose period it was not. The two three-bay wings on either side of the main block had shell motifs over the windows. He'd used cheap limestone and covered it with stucco. Both were, by Nick's time, crumbling. Inside in the best Soane manner the light came from odd places and staircases and doors were not predictable. An unwary guest could easily get lost and even the family might sometimes be blinded by a shaft of light from an unexpected dome and, for a moment, lose their orientation.

Nick's growth to manhood had brought with it the feeling that he ought to do something to maintain the house. In so far as he had a picture of himself it was as a son of, and therefore responsible for, this beautiful, decrepit object. His father, Randolph Trimming, ninth baronet, had given up the struggle. He'd become a writer, then a journalist, then a poet, then, really, nothing. Nick could just remember his father, battling with the responsibilities, the bills, the decisions, then, as Randolph realised he could not remedy or cope with them, he'd retreated into posing, excluding, denying and cutting out the world. He dwelt, apparently quite happily, amidst the chaos of the central wing, rarely penetrating beyond the piano nobile. Nick saw his father's life sometimes as a series of stops and checks beyond which he could not go. Like an insect in a maze, Randolph would butt up against some problem which would force him to change course. The roof of the west wing fell in when Nick was twelve. Randolph had simply moved what he could rescue of the furniture out and never gone there again. In his career, when it became obvious that his friends in the BBC World Service were no longer going to take his occasional pieces, he'd called himself a poet and bothered them no more. Nick did not know whether he admired his father for his realism or reviled him for his lack of perseverance. But as he reached his teens and began to detect in himself the same lack of talent and feared the same lack of perseverance, he clung the more tightly to the idea that something must be done with the only thing which redeemed them both: the house.

He wondered sometimes if it might have been possible to do something effective if his mother had stayed. He remembered her as an intense and turbulent presence given to hysteria. She had an untrammelled energy that seemed constantly to be fighting what the house was and what the Trimmings were or anyway had, by the time of Randolph, become. When Nick was six, she had left. She'd been a collected piece from Argentina. There she must have been commonplace. In England she appeared exotic. Randolph had chosen her, Nick came to suspect, on the same principle that people select souvenirs from foreign parts. A row of similar images may look vulgar when stacked all together in a shop window, but the hope is, if they are removed from their companions they may acquire quality. In Margaretta's case, Nick gathered from gossip scarcely bothered to be concealed in his presence, she had no quality to bring out. When it became apparent to her that she had not married money, only debts and a title that conferred nothing in the way of her sort of power, she'd left for a life of fabulous riches with an American dentist. Sometimes she sent Nick a postcard. When Nick had conceived his scheme, his life work, to restore the house, he'd written and asked her for money. There had been no reply. So then he had taken to his life of crime.

Nick sat on the edge of the tank and let his legs dangle over the edge. He sought out such small gestures of freedom since his time in prison. He wondered if he remembered when it had been full of dark green water with lily leaves undulating on the surface or whether he'd constructed the picture from what plausibly could have been. He gazed towards the stables. The stables were a museum, indeed a graveyard of Randolph's attempts to generate cash. The empty fish tanks indicated the koi carp breeding phase; the rotting pots of mouldy compost dated from the time when it had seemed possible to sell aspidistras to the local garden centre. But the fashion for them had passed and the growths, amazingly, in that well-nigh indestructible plant, had not been healthy.

Nick found his teeth were chattering with cold. He'd not eaten since breakfast with his father at Laddy's by Highcliffe station. He reckoned he couldn't eat again before supper, otherwise they'd run out of bread before tomorrow's breakfast. On the other hand after supper he'd need to be alert. They had a meeting, him and Jason, and the fat guy in a blue suit who drove a Merc and whose name he knew only as Dave. It was the last meeting before the run. Nick loved these meetings before the run when he felt himself valued and part of the firm. When the run was finished and they'd all gone he'd be given his cut. He fixed his mind on the cut. Five K. He wondered if he dared ring Jason, just for reassurance. He liked to hear the glottal tones and the streetwise remarks. Jason knew he'd been in prison and didn't care. In fact it gave him status.

Nick entered the house through the stable-yard entrance and stopped inside the door. The scullery, stone-flagged and stone-basined, smelled of drains. He listened, then went to the cupboard behind the old iron range. From far back on the top shelf he fumbled down a mobile phone. He'd put it there so Randolph could not use it. Randolph got dizzy if he had to put his arms above his head. Nick was immensely proud of the phone. Jason had given it to him when he'd had to reveal that the house was not on the phone; or, to be more accurate, had been cut off some time ago. Jason was shocked, not by the fact of being cut off, which was commonplace in his circle too, but by Nick being so unenterprising as not to have remedied the matter by picking up, that is, stealing, a replacement. Jason couldn't understand Nick's hesitation. Nick had stolen cars readily enough, hadn't he? He'd been inside, hadn't he? He knew what life was really like. You had to look out for yourself. Why shouldn't you have what you wanted if you could get it without reprisal?

In truth Jason found much that he couldn't understand about Nick and his father. That great big house, he'd asked Nick in the early days of their acquaintance, why not sell it and you'd be millionaires?

'No, no we couldn't do that.' Nick was helpless in the face of his own emotions. He didn't want to sell it. Anyway, as his father always said when he found himself enmeshed in this sort of conversation with relations or solicitors, who would buy it except some bounder? Some pop star on dope? 'It's mine, ours. We'll hang on.'

'Wouldn't the National Trust . . . ?' Nick had one day attempted to introduce some variant into this conversation with his father.

'Only if we could get enough together for an endowment.'
'What's an endowment?' Nick had asked.
'Biggish sum set aside for the maintenance of the fabric.'
'How big?' Nick had persisted.
'Oh, thousands, old man.' His father had fobbed him off, not because he despised his son but because he despised himself for having done so little about it.

But the notion had lodged in Nick's mind. It gave him a purpose. All he needed to make everything all right was thousands. So he'd set out to get his first thousand and met Jason in the course of so doing. He had learned his language too and by now was beginning to be fluent in it.

'Anyway,' Jason had concluded in the matter of the mobile phone, 'you'll need it in the trade. We'll want to ring you. Set times, like. So's to be sure.'

Nick clicked the familiar numbers and waited. Jason's voice, when it came, sounded hoarse and unfamiliar. 'Wha' you wan'?'

'Jas? Just wondered if there was any change. For tonight?'
'Change? Naw. Why would we?'
'You sound a bit stressed, Jas.'
'Can't talk. Bi' of bovver, like.'
'What sort of bovver, Jas?'
'Nothing we can't sort. Just a bi' ou' of order, like. Bloke 'ere go' himself done in.'
'How?'
'Tell you when I see you.'
'Buccaneer, ninish. Right?'
'Right.'
'See you.'
'Cheers.'

Nick considered how things lay. Who had got himself killed and how and why? He associated Bolly's Jolly Holiday Home with discomfort (Jason had taken him for a drink there once) but not actual violence. However, it was good to think about the meeting this evening. All he had to do now was find a way to pass six hours. He looked out at the by now sleeting rain. He listened again to the familiar sounds of the rotting house. His father must be having his afternoon nap. Stealthily Nick made his way from the kitchen up the back stairs, his trainers silent on the uncarpeted treads, until he reached the attic storey. Carefully he unlatched the door of what had once been the dormitory for the maids stretching over the whole width of the house. He looked at the long table in the middle and drew up a stool. It was an afternoon to play with the Meccano.

The Millennium Message Conference had not been plunged into disarray. The Bishop had been withdrawn from fraternising with the polloi at coffee break to be told that the dead body of a man, apparently murdered, had been found in a washing machine in the laundrette. Moreover and worse, the body had been recognised by the man who had found it, the Reverend Daniel Ripe, as one of the conference members, the jester priest, Joshua Makepeace. The police had been informed. Everyone was to remain calm. No one was to leave the site.

The Bishop remained calm and had no intention of leaving the site. It was his conference, his first in his new diocese, his first in episcopal orders. He was blessed if anything was going to stop him setting targets, getting things under way, making, above all, changes. He gathered Peach, Worsted and the Archdeacon. 'We must all remain calm,' said Worsted, unwisely taking the lead. His hands were trembling. Someone, he just knew it, was going to blame him for all this.

They were in the Warm Welcome office. With what he thought was true inspiration, Worsted had turned round the cardboard 'open' sign on the door to read 'closed'. He wished he'd thought to have a notice 'Conference in

Progress' made. Too late now. The story of his life. How could this have happened to him? He'd led a blameless existence.

'Nevertheless, we shall need to break the news to conference,' said Peach.

'And some members of the conference may just feel that once the police have made their inquiries, decorum would suggest we discontinue . . .' The Archdeacon caught sight of the Bishop's face and stopped.

'Decorum?' snorted the Bishop. 'What's decorum got to do with it? Our duty is plain before us. We are here to build up, to edify the Church in this diocese. We can't run off back to our kennels every time we meet a bit of misfortune.'

They all digested this. Misfortune, the Archdeacon thought, but did not say, is not the word I would have chosen. Indeed 'fortune' is a difficult concept for Christians to use, everything being in the hand of God.

'Still, you'll need a service,' Worsted said. 'Of some sort,' he limped on.

'We can pray, of course, and pray we will, but we can't have a burial before the body's released.' The Bishop drew on his worldly knowledge of such matters.

'When will that be?' An Archdeacon's role is to be smart on timetables.

'When the murderer's found.' Peach was inaccurate but had read a lot of detective fiction and felt he'd been here before, in imagination at least. 'It might be weeks or months or never.' He thought of a range of fiction titles where these eventualities had prevailed.

'I imagine there'll have to have an inquest.' The Archdeacon was still totting up timetables.

'What about the police?' Worsted asked, bravely putting into words his fears.

Here there was a battering sound and the glass of the door shook. Victor's face could be seen pressed to it. He made a series of hand signals which it took the assembled clergy a moment to interpret as turning a key. Peach let him in.

Victor's mentors would have been proud of him. He'd got a clipboard and a full list of all conference members. In addition he had a separate colour-coded list of the staff. He had a list of the rooms occupied, a list of police with ranks and telephone numbers and a timetable. He was replete with appropriate information. His air was one of quiet, elated confidence. Here was an opportunity to use all his talents at once. 'Crisis is what you live by, crises are what Bolly's never have,' he remembered from his two-week training course at Bolly's HQ. Next year Skegness. Birmingham Conference Centre and the challenge of the Japanese beckoned.

'I'm sorry to interrupt you, Bishop, gentlemen, but the Superintendent is busy, as you can imagine. He asked me if I'd let you know the arrangements.'

The Bishop wasn't sure he wanted other people commanding the arrangements but he let it pass, confident of his ability to ignore or subvert them in the future if he judged that necessary.

'The incident room . . .' Victor began. He'd never said it before. It sounded good. He said it again. 'The incident room is Harries Bar.' He waved his hand across Main Street. 'They're bringing their own computers. The ladies' lounge will be the interview room.'

'Which Superintendent?' The Archdeacon had been in post a long time. He'd served three Bishops. He knew anyone of any importance in the county.

'Superintendent Spruce of Medwich CID is in charge of the case. He and Inspector Tilby will personally see every member of the staff and all conference members to check times and places. They're beginning now with the domestic staff.'

Victor hoped that he wasn't going to be given notice by too many of these in the near future. In this he misread human nature. A murder attracts people, it does not repel them. He was more likely to be able to fill cleaning posts in the next few weeks than he might have been in the season.

'When was . . . when was he killed?' the Archdeacon asked abruptly.

Victor hesitated but the status conferred by knowledge triumphed over professionalism. 'Sometime yesterday evening. Monday. It's hard to tell owing to the temperature apparently. From the washing machines.'

The Archdeacon shuddered. He turned his mind away from this ungainly death. 'Have the police any idea about the motive or who killed him?'

'That, I'm afraid, I could not say.' Victor was genuinely regretful. He would have loved to have been able to hint.

'Have the family been informed?'

'That I couldn't tell you.'

'What's he got?' The Bishop felt left out of the conversation.

'He has a father somewhere out Felixstowe way, I believe. Beyond that I'm not sure.' It was Worsted who knew. He'd had to engage the fellow for the conference.

'The Superintendent said he particularly wants to talk early on to anyone who knew him well.'

'Canon Oldsalmon might know him,' said the Archdeacon. 'Makepeace was of the Catholic wing and there may be others, of course. He's had a ministry in jesting . . . of this sort for several years.'

Victor found Canon Oldsalmon on his list and drew a circle round it. 'Oh, and the Superintendent said not to break the conference up but to find some way of keeping it going because it'll be easier to pursue inquiries that way.'

The Bishop looked up in triumph. 'Just what I said. Tell the Superintendent we're not going to give in. We shall soldier on. With decorum, of course.' He looked at the Archdeacon with distaste.

Superintendent Spruce rocked on his heels in Harries Bar, his elbows on the counter facing across the room. A team of support staff hurried in and out carrying computers and faxes. This was his first case in his new promotion.

'It has all the makings.' He spoke out loud.

His inspector looked at him. They'd worked together before. Each knew and forgave the other's qualities.

'I mean, it has its piquancies,' Spruce went on.

This use of language was one of the things Inspector Tilby forgave Superintendent Spruce. Spruce would not go higher in the force because he used words like that. He was sensitive and knowledgeable in all sorts of areas where he shouldn't be. He wasn't *educated*. Tilby didn't have to forgive him that. He wasn't one of these university coppers. He'd left school at seventeen and done a year with the police cadets before entering the force. No, his difficulty, Inspector Tilby reckoned, was that he picked things up: knowledge, people, words were his meat and drink. He turned them over in his mind and, if they fitted his needs, he adapted and used them. It was unnerving at times. You didn't know where you were with him, what he might not come up with. That made his seniors uneasy. The police like everything to be nice and predictable, Spruce had said. He knew his own faults as well as any.

But for Tilby Spruce was all right. His eccentricities weren't used to belittle but out of relish for the first hand and the original. Tilby knew Spruce to be resourceful, energetic and dedicated. It was the slapdash, careless, slothful incompetence of the average criminal, Inspector Tilby had come to realise, which angered Spruce. He hated success going where it was not deserved. The only time Tilby had seen Spruce at all reluctant to close in was with a forger named George Allbright for whose skill in constructing driving licences and import documents for stolen goods Spruce's admiration had been evident. Allbright was a careful, hardworking man, Spruce reckoned. It was a terrible waste of such qualities to put him in prison for four years.

Tilby, who had himself been born and schooled in Medwich, felt at ease with another local lad, who knew Medwich, its villains, both convicted and unconvicted, in high places as well as low, its virtues as well as its vices. Nevertheless, he recognised that what made Spruce a good policeman, this magpie faculty, this relish for and openness to the nuances of societies not his own, would bar his promotion. No provincial force was going to make an Assistant Chief Constable of someone who used 'piquancies'. Of that Tilby was certain.

'Do you think they like it, appreciate it, eh?' Spruce addressed his colleague.

'How do you mean?' Tilby was cautious.

'The clergy, in this tin pot decaying hell hole, as the setting for a conference of those dedicated to changing the world.' Spruce waved his hand in the direction of the dilapidated fruit machines of antique pattern.

'Eh? I thought they were clergy, not politicians.'

'Different sort of change, but change nonetheless.'

'One less to do it now.' Tilby indicated the growing mound of computer printouts.

'True. Well then. Come on. Let's get to it. What have we got so far? Start with the victim. Read it back.'

Tilby gathered up a length of printout and began to read. 'The dead man was a forty-eight-year-old Caucasian male in good physical condition. Five foot eight, ten stone, well developed pectoral and thigh muscles. Dark brown hair going grey, worn shortish in an army cut. Gold earring in left ear.'

'Brings him vividly before me,' Spruce remarked.

Tilby looked up from his script, 'Knew him, did you?'

'No. Keep going. Clothe him in reality.'

'The deceased has been identified as the Reverend Henry Joshua Makepeace, born Medwich 1950. City of Medwich School, London College of Art and Design 1968 to '71. Then took a short service commission with the Royal Navy '71 to '76.'

'Parents?' Spruce prompted as though he might know the answer to his own query.

'Henry Joshua Makepeace, Captain RN. Now, of course, retired. Lives out at—'

'Bradan Bank,' Spruce chipped in. 'Owns a small boatyard on the estuary.'

'Has he got some form?' Tilby couldn't imagine Spruce knowing anyone if they hadn't.

'Not so far as I know. I used to do a bit of frost-biting round the Broadwater and he coached idiots like me.'

'Explains his son's naval inclinations. Short service commission. He didn't make a life of it like his dad. Didn't do as well really.'

'Depends what you think about the importance of the clergy.'

Tilby had the sense not to be drawn on this one with Spruce.

'Go on.' Spruce would have quite liked Tilby's views on this one but could see he wasn't going to get them. 'Does his father know?'

'We told him,' Tilby looked at his watch, 'a couple of hours ago. He'll be identifying him in Felixstowe mortuary about now.'

'There is no possible mistake about the identity?'

'Not really. That bloke who found him, Ripe, Reverend Daniel Ripe, knew him as a fellow priest. Reckoned he'd seen him on a number of previous occasions.'

'So we'll have to see his dad.'

'I said this evening. That's right, isn't it?'

Spruce nodded. That was always the bit he hated. But then only a sadist would have enjoyed that part of the job. Puzzle solving, hunting down, ticking off possibilities as they were exhausted and discarded until you got down to the one explanation which could possibly fit, that sort of pragmatic analysis he loved. So now he nodded. 'Yes, that's right. I'll go down this evening.'

Tilby knew it would be. He knew too just how very good at that difficult task Spruce would be. His humanity was another thing which would stop him going further up the ladder.

'Has he any brothers or sisters?'

Tilby conned his list. 'Nope. Or anyway not traced down. And he wasn't married either.'

'So what about the rest of his career? What brought him to this unhappy pass?'

'Well, there's a very useful book on the clergy's careers.' Tilby was smug. 'It's called—'

'Crockford,' Spruce said. And thought of all the scores of clergy he was going to have to interview for this case, all with their little paragraphs in Crockford.

'Right. Well, Crockford says he was trained for the priesthood at Cuddesdon 1978 to '81. Deaconed in Medwich cathedral 1982, priested 1984. Curate St James's, Felixstowe, extra chaplain Felixstowe Polytechnic '81 to '90. That would be the new university. Lectured in extra-mural studies in the Craft and Technological Studies department.'

Bright boy, or were they desperate for cheap teaching help? Spruce wondered. 'Then what?'

'Resigned from the parish and chaplaincy 1990 and all goes quiet as far as the good book is concerned.'

'So do we know how he makes a living?'

'Preliminary inquiries suggest,' Tilby began formally, 'that is, the clergy we've been able to interview so far say that he makes a living as a jester.' Tilby looked embarrassed.

'Yes,' said Spruce thoughtfully, 'yes that's exactly what I've heard tell of him.'

'So what does he do? You tell me.'

'He juggles, makes jokes, visual ones, tumbles, mimes and mimics.'

'In a circus,' Tilby hazarded.

'No, in church.'

'Like for a children's party.'

'That's it. That's exactly it. Only for Christians, for Church people.'

'Why?'

'To amuse, to take people out of their blinkers. To make them think. Hold a mirror up to nature. Every institution needs one. We could do with one in the force.'

'And that's how he knocked out a living?'

'Apparently. However . . .' Spruce paused and stared at one of the old fruit machines which had suddenly and mysteriously lurched into life over the far side of the bar. 'However, there is the question of what he did between '76 and '78.'

'Leaving the Navy and studying for the priesthood.'

'And perhaps again between leaving Felixstowe University chaplaincy and starting up as a freelance jester.'

'There was a gap then?'

'Canon Oldsalmon says no one seems to remember him in this diocese before about 1995.'

'Case of the appearing and disappearing jester.'

'Perhaps his dad will know.'

'Perhaps.'

'And finally' – Tilby looked down at the remains of his printout – 'the actual killing. He died from a single stab wound which went straight through his heart delivered from behind with a lot of strength.'

'And knowledge.'

'And knowledge,' Tilby agreed. 'Or a lot of luck, if it was a fluke.'

'Weapon?'

'Forensic say two-edged knife with a longish point. We haven't found it yet.'

'Not common.'

'Not common. Butchers sometimes, also Army combat weapons.'

'Also naval combat weapons,' Spruce said carefully.

'That's it,' Tilby concluded. 'How do you want to play it?'

Spruce looked round the unlikely setting and deeply inhaled the stench of stale beer and cigarettes. 'Can you stay on?'

Tilby was a married man with a young family. Spruce was considerate of such things. Tilby was appreciative. That was another reason why he was happy to work with Spruce. It was not just that he could surprise by what he knew, it was also that he valued his colleagues as though (Tilby put it to himself) they were real to him, not just weapons to get the job done or further his own career. 'Yes, Pam's taken the kids to their nan's for the week. Nice breath of polluted city air she reckons'll do them the world of good.'

Spruce grinned. 'We'll give it all we've got for the next forty-eight hours. We'll take half the interview list each and just keep going.' He looked at his watch. It was three o'clock. 'Till sevenish. Then we'll have a bit of supper and I'll drive over to see the father round eight. Right?'

'Right.'

'Get that young hopeful, the manager, Victor something, to do us a round of sarnies. Get that finicky sergeant of yours to put all the statements so far on a computer and run them for us as soon as we've done them.'

'How about the press?'

'Anything with clergy in it makes the nationals but there's no reason why we shouldn't give our local lads a bit beforehand. Ring Timson on the *Eastern Evening News* and tell them there'll be a press conference tomorrow night here six p.m.'

Spruce paused and looked at his list. There was a knock at the door. Victor put his head round. 'There's sarnies and coffee, if you'd like. And you said you'd like to see early anyone who knew the deceased personally. Well, apart from Canon Oldsalmon, whom I think you have seen, there's Reverend Worsted.'

Spruce gazed at the youth with appreciation. 'That's very good of you, Victor. On the house, would they be?'

'On the house,' said Victor grandly.

CHAPTER FOUR

Trailing the Jester

Lucy Royal patted Theodora's arm. 'My dear, such a long time. Arthur said when he saw the programme: "If Theo's going to speak, it'll be worth hearing. We must make the effort." So we packed up our TSK, travel-to-survive kit, you know, and came along.'

'I'm not sure I'm going to be worth the trouble,' said Theodora, 'but the conference looks as though it might be interesting.' She stopped, conscious of the implications. Sometimes a scholarly interest can look like flippancy. Father Raymond Sentinel's grim old skull relaxed into something like a smile. The lunch table in the Splendide Diner was animated. It couldn't be said that the death of the jester priest had subdued the spirits. No one actually mentioned the dead man. No one actually said that there was a murderer at large, but the unspoken thought released energy into the assembly all the same.

The Bishop's short announcement, the prayers delivered by the Archdeacon and therefore appropriate and sincere (that is, decorous), the Bishop's own subsequent rallying cry of business as usual, phrased as 'our duty to follow where the Spirit moves us, onwards and upwards as our brother would have wished', all left the conference-goers with the feeling of rising to a challenge. Some of them, indeed, were old enough to remember the Dunkirk spirit: a spirit which, Theodora noticed, had a measure of self-congratulation about it.

The Splendide Diner held a hundred and fifty clergy and laity laying into a purplish mess of ham and boiled potatoes. It reminded many of school lunches, and like the good men and women that they were, they treated it as punishment rather than nourishment. The Bishop's chaplain had said grace and spoke of gratitude and many genuinely tried to summon that emotion.

There was a certain amount of *réclame* attending those whom the police had already interviewed. 'What are they asking?' Father Raymond inquired. Theodora could have told them.

'"Did you know the dead man personally or by reputation? When did you last see him alive? When did you arrive at Bolly's? Can you prove that time? What were you doing between the hours of six and eight?" That sort of thing,' said the young priest whom Theodora recognised as the man who had been introduced as new to the diocese, the ex-naval gunner, Father Martin Guard.

'And *did* you know him?' asked Arthur.

For a moment it seemed to Theodora that the young man hesitated then he said, 'Actually we served on *The Prometheus* together my first trip. I didn't know him well. He was ten years senior to me, already a lieutenant. Later I heard he'd taken orders.'

He sounded slightly resentful, as though it was unfair that more than one, and that one himself, should have become priests from that background. She weighed up his answer. Her only knowledge of the Navy came to her via her vicar, the Reverend Geoffrey Brighouse, who had also seen service in the Navy after Cambridge and before being priested. His words came back to her. 'The worst part is being cooped up with the same hundred-odd men for three months at a time. You get to know people far too well.' Had Father Guard known Joshua Makepeace far too well?

Father Raymond clearly felt the need to turn the conversation. He pushed his plate from him and gave his energy to the company. He smiled at Arthur Royal. 'It is Dr Royal, isn't it? We met briefly at the caucus of African Missionary Societies. You spoke most movingly of your work in East Africa.'

Arthur's brown shrivelled face smiled back at him. 'In the middle of such turmoil and, at times, terror it seems ungrateful to say that I believe Lucy and I have had such blessed, such genuinely happy lives.'

Lucy moved the mashed potatoes in his direction. 'Arthur dear, you know we said we must resist the temptation to dwell in the past. The present is what matters. What are we going to do—?' She broke off. Theodora wondered what she was going to say. She followed Lucy's gaze but could not pinpoint its object which was on the other side of the room. Arthur too turned to look in that direction. There was no one except the innocent broad back of Canon Oldsalmon disappearing through the door.

'There is always evil to combat,' she said, 'and we all need to pull together to overcome it. We can't do it alone.' It sounded like a generalised comment but it might have been addressed to Father Raymond Sentinel.

'What's the programme for the afternoon?' he inquired.

'Well, I understand the police are going on with their questioning. There are over a hundred of us. But we're going to go to the study group on' – Lucy fumbled the programme from her handbag – '"The Challenge of Change in the Parish Setting, a Youth Presentation". Chris Teane is leading it. He always seems such a vigorous young man, full of ideas about how to bring youth in and keep them happy until they're old enough to see the point of things.'

'Lucy means until they can be taught to appreciate the Prayer Book and its collects and understand the disciplines of the religious life.' Arthur smiled fondly on his wife.

'They have to have a certain number of years between fifteen and twenty-five playing ping-pong and listening to records before they come to understand about eternity.' Lucy was not censorious. She might have been describing the ritual habits of an African tribe.

'Not records, dear, nowadays it's discs.'

'What's the difference?'

'Small, silver, no needle. But the sound's the same, only louder. What are *you* going to do, Father?' Arthur smiled at Father Sentinel.

'I'm going to have an afternoon nap,' he said firmly. 'Then I shall read St John to prepare myself for tomorrow's lecture by the young man from Felixstowe.'

'I'm going to that bank manager chap, layman, Cave, Ray Cave, on "Financial Planning in the Parish Setting",' Father Martin Guard offered.

'I thought I'd give that one a glance too.' The Archdeacon wasn't pompous but he knew his presence would set a seal of approval on any group. 'Forty years with Lloyds must give him some sort of a grasp of how to cope with the average parish income of three thousand a year.'

'They never seem to put on anything about *diocesan* financial planning. It's always "in the parish setting".'

Was Arthur innocent or was he stirring it? Theodora wondered.

'We wouldn't dare.' The Archdeacon was honest.

'All those new computers, all those additional secretaries. All that new office space.' Father Raymond's skeletal face was almost flushed.

'The Bishop calls it casting bread on waters.' The

Archdeacon had to stick up for the central administration.

'Bureaucratic self-aggrandisement,' said Sentinel with feeling. 'Enhancing the egos of the office boys. All done on the pennies of the poor people in the pew.'

Theodora grinned. Medwich was not or anyway was not any longer her diocese. She'd done a spell there in her youth attached to the cathedral but it sounded as though things hadn't changed. She was about to say as much when a face appeared behind her chair. She recognised the young man from the management. Victor said, 'Superintendent Spruce wondered if you could spare him a moment, miss?'

He hadn't changed that much, Theodora thought. He looked as fresh and nimble as he had ten years ago. His gymnast's agility didn't seem diminished. His hair had gone dark grey early but his thick black brows suggested energy unextinguished. He rose as she came in and offered a hand across the beer-ringed table in Harries Bar. Surrounded by the winking lights of the ancient fruit machines, they shook hands, delighted to see each other.

'Miss Braithwaite, Theodora, Theo,' Spruce said, taking up where they had left off ten years ago. 'It's been a long time.'

'You've prospered, Superintendent.' Theodora was as glad as he.

'You're not the first woman bishop?'

'I'm not even in priest's orders.'

'Because?'

'Oh because. You know. Power. People – women want it because they think priesthood's linked to political-type power, which the Church shouldn't be about.' Theodora stopped. That wasn't why she was here. 'I can be very boring on the subject.'

'Impossible,' said Spruce with that mixture of irony and sincerity which she'd found so attractive ten years ago.

'However, *you* have risen.'

'Only recently,' Spruce admitted. 'This is my first case in my new rank.'

'So you've got to succeed with it.'

'Unlike you I'm not immune to worldly ambition. I like a bit of success now and again. Good for the ego, good for the criminals, lets them know there's' – he was going to say 'a God in Heaven', but he changed it – 'justice in a wicked world.'

'So here and now?'

'You were very helpful last time, in the case of Hereward Marr.'

'And now you have another dead priest.'

'Different though. Every case is different. But the clergy remain the same.'

'I suppose we do.'

'It has its strength.'

'It may look like that from the outside,' Theodora conceded. 'From the inside it can breed frustration.'

'In this particular case, I was wondering—' Spruce stopped.

'Naturally, any help I can give from my amateur status . . .' Theodora came to his aid.

Spruce sighed. 'I'd really be most grateful. It's a clerical crime, and as far as we've been able to determine so far, it's motiveless. Not a strong start.' He looked up at Theodora. 'Did you by any chance know him?'

Theodora recalled the bright morning light of a London church in summer and the figure of Joshua weaving in and out of a fashionable congregation. 'Just. That is, I've seen his act, his jesting, once. And I know his reputation, which isn't confined to Medwich diocese.'

'What's it about, would you say?'

'He's a professional intruder. He interrupts things, services, meetings, to try to get people to stop and think.'

Spruce nodded. 'Go on.'

'He preaches as well but mainly he's physical. He's dextrous. He juggles. Like satirists in political society, so a jester with physical action can comment, can make a point in clerical society. I mean, we, the clergy, do communicate by gesture. Even the Evangelicals use a lot of body language. He was good at parodying that.'

'That's a very helpful description. I never saw him myself but he did a thing at my lad's school. Tim said he was brilliant, or as he put it, "brill".'

'And now he's dead.'

'Yes.'

'Are the two things, his death and his jesting, connected?' Theodora asked.

'That's what we need to discover. Was he, would you say, liked, I mean by his fellow clergy?' Spruce asked.

Theodora considered. 'Yes, on the whole, I'd say he was. Well, perhaps it's truer to say that where he was liked he was liked very much.'

'Did you like him?'

'The little I saw of him, yes. He punctured self-regard and pomposity without malice and that's quite a gift.'

'Would everyone see it that way?'

'I can see that many would find him irritating and some might find him threatening. But he never went to perform anywhere unless invited and he made it clear beforehand what he'd be doing.'

'Could his act have led to someone hating or fearing him so much that they'd want to kill him?'

'Surely only a madman.'

Spruce sighed. The interesting bit was concluded for him and it merely confirmed what he thought. Now he'd need to return to routine. 'Did you know his family?'

'Not at all.'

'Or his contacts, friends, colleagues?'

'He was alone in his art. My feeling is he didn't have close friends.'

'I feared as much.'

'I believe he had a father who lives or perhaps lived locally.'

Spruce grasped at it. 'He's alive. I'm going over this evening. He's out towards Broadwater. Has a boatyard. I suppose you wouldn't care to . . . ?'

'If I can be of help.'

'We're short of women police at the moment and they usually do that sort of bereavement-counselling role.' Spruce stopped, aware of having waded into deeper waters than he intended. He tried to recoup. 'Not that I'm lining you up with women PCs. And anyway it's not that women PCs or women don't have equal roles . . . political correctness and all that.' He broke off, realising that he was not doing too well.

'Right,' said Theodora, who had no truck with either women or political correctness as concepts. She had no sense of self-importance and was therefore almost impossible to insult. 'Don't worry, I'll willingly come along and give any help I can to the father.'

Spruce looked hugely pleased with himself. 'I'll be leaving about half-seven. Pick you up outside Warm Welcome?'

'It's a bit public for a pick-up. Are you sure you want the whole of the Anglican communion to know I'm helping the police with their inquiries?'

Spruce recognised he'd missed a trick. 'The first pub outside the camp is The Buccaneer, left-hand side before the lights.'

'Right,' said Theodora and prepared to depart.

Spruce intercepted. 'Look, I'm awfully sorry but I'm going to have to ask you some duty questions – just for the record, as we say. When did you come and so on.'

'Of course.' Theodora settled again into the rickety bar-parlour chair in the evil-smelling den.

Slowly they made their way down the list. Finally Spruce asked (a question which was not on his duty list), 'Why did you come? I mean, this isn't your diocese, is it, as I understand it?'

'You may well ask,' Theodora agreed. 'I was invited to give a paper on women's ministry.'

Spruce tried to look interested. 'So you came down from London this morning and you're staying till it finishes on Saturday and then going back.'

'No. I'm going to look up some relations before I go back to London.'

'Who would they be?'

'The Trimmings out at Wrackheath.'

Spruce raised his eyes. 'Close relations?'

'No. Quite distant. But as families go we keep in touch.'

Theodora thought of her Great-uncle Hugh, retired Canon of Ely, who as head of the family, kept himself alive by gingering up the rest of them from his fenland retreat. Cards, at regular intervals, for birthdays, and, in the case of the clerical members of the family, for anniversaries of ordination, dropped through letter boxes the length and breadth of England. At his command Braithwaites by birth and marriage gathered for reunion in inconvenient parts of the country after the major Christian festivals.

Theodora's father, Nicholas Braithwaite, who had died too young in a living on the outskirts of Oxford, had made sure that Theodora knew the family. Her mother, who had died before she was seven, would, he used to say, have wished it. Theodora sometimes wondered whether this was true. Her mother, she suspected, might have found the Braithwaites a dull, conventional lot. Many were clergy, some were civil servants. There was a sprinkling of professional soldiers. Her mother's family, on the other hand, had thrown up the odd opera singer, a daring mathematician or two from a background of downwardly mobile Celtic aristocracy. They were less censorious, less smug than her father's clan. For this reason alone she felt some sympathy with Randolph Trimming.

However, Theodora was dutiful. Dutifully, therefore, she had acquiesced in her father's arrangements for her. She went each summer to some new relation for part of the school holidays. Hence she was familiar with large tracts of the south coast and the East Anglian fens. From such holidays too she had learned to fit in, to please, to be adaptable, to observe, to keep her own counsel. No bad training for the diaconate, she thought. Nor, indeed, the Superintendent might have added, for a detective.

She was never sure whether in these childhood excursions she was offering herself on her own account or whether she was representing her father. He, for sure, preferred to linger at home in his beloved parish, which he hated leaving. Now she had a parish of her own, albeit shared with her vicar, she knew how he felt. When at last she was old enough and free enough to choose where she could go for holidays she was surprised to find herself still swayed by the old compulsions. She had continued to carry out her father's wishes about her family obligations. She stood godmother to and entertained cousins at the ultimate degree of kinship. She was not therefore surprised to receive her marching orders from Uncle Hugh.

Canon Hugh had first sent a card and then telephoned when Nicholas Trimming had been caught in a stolen car on the outskirts of Felixstowe. 'See what you can do for them,' he'd said. 'Randolph was always wayward,' he'd added. 'He has neglected the proper education of his son. I think the lad ended up in some sort of local elementary school, where doubtless he kept bad company.'

Theodora, who had as a child equated the pronouncements of Canon Hugh with those of the Old

Testament God, did not challenge the many assumptions which she did not share. At least her own career had not suffered such parental neglect. Her own progression had indeed been one of exemplary Braithwaitian dullness. Cheltenham had been followed by Oxford, ordination had been preceded by Cuddesdon. She had never given the family an ounce of worry.

She read Canon Hugh's card for the address and wrote briefly to Randolph reminding him of the kindness he had shown her when she was fourteen and on holiday at Lowestoft. Could she, she hesitantly suggested, look in since she was conferencing at Highcliffe in a month's time. There had been no reply. She had tried telephoning but apparently Wrackheath was no longer a subscriber. She rang Father Sentinel, recently retired to the parish of Wrackheath, who had said, 'Leave it with me.' The result of that had been a note on thin lined blue paper saying:

Do drop by if you want. I'm terribly busy these days so if I'm not around I expect Nick will entertain you. I hope your father's well.

Love, RT

Since her father had died three years ago Theodora knew Randolph was in bad case.

So now, four days before her projected visit to Wrackheath and engaged ostensibly on quite other business, she raised her eyes and looked at Superintendent Spruce and asked. 'Are the Trimmings *known*?'

'Had the boy in for nicking cars. You probably know. He'd been at it some time. He's a silly little beggar. He never did anything with them. Just good at picking locks and starting them. Drove them around a bit and then left them as often as not and walked home. After he'd been doing it a bit a patrol car stumbled on him carefully relocking a Merc outside Felixstowe docks and preparing to catch the bus back to Highcliffe. He was in Medwich jail on remand for six weeks, which had its effect,' Spruce concluded with relish. 'He got community service for a first offence and seventeen other counts to be taken into consideration. He spent a happy couple of months painting school classrooms, I believe.'

'Not a villain?'

'Not altogether there in the top storey, I'd say. Trouble is, of course, when you get someone like that, cleverer lads start to use his talents.'

'Has that happened?'

'He goes around with one or two bad boys who do a bit of this, bit of that. He really ought to get right away from here. Get some training, get a living in his hands. I gather his dad can't afford to do anything for him and he hasn't the sense to do anything for himself.'

Theodora thought that that was exactly what she'd imagined. And it was her duty, Canon Hugh had intimated, to see something of the sort happened.

Lucy Royal picked her way purposefully through the afternoon tea throng in The OK Corale conference room towards Canon Oldsalmon. She was no longer quick in her movements but she wasn't frail either. Firm of purpose was firm of step. Canon Oldsalmon kept disappearing from view amongst the crowds gathered for refreshment after the effort of the afternoon's work groups. His was an ample figure but he had the nimbleness of a tubby man. When she did finally catch up with him, she was for a moment breathless.

'Charles, I looked for you at lunch but you didn't show.'

'I was a shade late in. I had a snifter with . . .' He stopped as old habits censored him '. . . an old Mirfield chum.'

The Canon had known the Royals for forty years but few laymen were intimate with him. He really felt safe only with fellow priests. A habit of reserve acquired in relation to the confessional in his first parish sometimes left him without casual conversation when it came to lay people. Not that he didn't trust Lucy, but he'd noticed that, since her retirement from the mission field, she'd found an outlet for her missionary instincts by taking up causes. Her friends allowed for energy, goodwill and sound organising abilities, but sometimes found her wish to coerce their help for (often) African causes, hospital beds in the Sahara, scholarships and sponsorships for this or that deserving youngster, exhausting.

'How's Medwich?' he inquired to stave off further revelations on his own part.

The Royals had retired to a cottage off the cathedral close. It allowed Arthur to worship amidst the cathedral's beauties and take duty as a steward and sidesman; it gave Lucy entrée into the cathedral's network, half policy, half gossip. Together they knew everything, she everybody. The life of quiet piety, after a career of turbulent effort, satisfied them both but just occasionally Lucy felt the spirit of enterprise stifled by the tranquillity of the close. It was an intimation of death that she intended to fight for a little while yet. Now she was intent on something. Canon Oldsalmon feared to know what.

'I need to talk to you.'

Canon Oldsalmon drew back almost physically. 'I'm not sure it's a good idea to chatter about poor Joshua's death,' he began.

'That's not what I want to talk about. Or not at least directly. It's the Bishop's photographs mix-up, the slides.'

'Ah yes, poor man.'

'It's obvious, isn't it, by his reactions that they'd been spiked.' Lucy's diction was not of the most modern. Nevertheless she shared a language as well as presuppositions of value and manner with the Canon. 'The question is why and by whom? Has he spoken to you about it?'

Canon Oldsalmon refrained from stating the obvious: that he was not, as an old, nearly retired, reactionary country priest, in the confidence of the utterly modern pushy Bishop, whose churchmanship, in any case, he did not share.

'He seemed to blame poor Peach rather,' Oldsalmon offered to placate the importunate woman.

'For what? For having pornographic slides and mixing them with his own?'

'Well no, I gather he felt Peach should have kept a tighter watch on them.'

'So he does think they were got at?' Lucy went on ferreting away.

'It seems obvious someone did.'

'I repeat, who and why?'

Canon Oldsalmon shook his fine Roman head.

'I'll tell you what I think.'

Canon Oldsalmon had feared as much. He scanned the emptying room in hope of a rescuer. Lucy edged him nearer the wall to prevent escape.

'I think it's part of a plot to compromise the Bishop's plans for change. I hear a lot, you know' – Canon Oldsalmon did not doubt it – 'and about a month ago I heard from an old friend of ours from the Africa Mission Co-ordinating Group. He said he'd heard of something called Adjumentum Salvatoris. Have you heard of it?'

Canon Oldsalmon looked uncomfortable.

'It's a Broederbond,' said Lucy. 'Men only,' she explained. 'There were a lot in South Africa. Like Masonic only religious.'

'What would that have to do with the Bishop's mixed slides?'

'They are not for the evangelicals.'

'But beggaring up slides would be childish.'

'Linking the Bishop with pornography might not be. Sling enough mud and some will stick.'

'I can't believe . . .'

'What number are you?'

'What?'

'Chalet number.'

'Two four eight.'

'Arthur and I are two fifty.'

'How very nice. We must . . . must . . .' Must what, he wondered.

'Were you here last night?'

'Yes. Actually I came down in the morning. A fact which the police seem to suppose lines me up as chief suspect. Apparently I would have been on site when Joshua was killed.'

Lucy was not pursuing the trail. 'And did you sleep soundly?'

'Yes, thank you. I generally have no trouble in that department.'

'Well, I didn't sleep too soundly. I heard voices. Plotting voices.'

'Plotting what?'

'Chaos,' said Lucy.

'I hope you aren't missing anything important?'

'Nothing is more important than murder, is it?'

Spruce was eager to speak of the crime, Theodora could feel. It might be a relief to him to talk to someone outside the case but familiar with the landscape in which it had taken place. They had after all collaborated in that way once before. 'Do you know yet where Joshua was killed?'

Spruce circumnavigated the main roundabout of the town just beyond The Buccaneer. He had been late for the pick-up. He'd had an altercation with Jason on the gate who pretended he didn't know who he was and wasn't going to let him out. Spruce wasn't too sure whether Jason was genuinely stupid or was playing silly beggars. He'd had to set him right about one or two things. Now he settled down to lay out the case before another and, he would have been the first to admit it, equal intelligence and see what they could together construct. Spruce leaned forward and switched the heater up a notch. It was a large Rover and the huge blast of air swept round the car efficiently.

'He was killed on site but not in the laundrette. Probably on the children's playground just the other side of the path.'

'How do you know?'

'Sand in his shoes matches the sand in the kiddies sandpit. Also blood and hair on the climbing apparatus. He was struck from behind, fell forward and was caught by the frame before he fell.'

'Why should anyone put him in a washing machine in the laundrette? Why not in an empty chalet?'

'Perhaps he, the murderer – let's assume it was a he – wasn't familiar with the place and didn't know where the chalets were.'

'Or perhaps they *were* familiar with the place and knew that conference members would be blundering in and out of chalets all evening.'

'Right. And the laundrette is the nearest private place to the playground and it would be reasonable to suppose that no conference-goer was going to arrive and want to do their washing straight away.'

'Reckoning without Daniel Ripe.' Theodora grinned. She'd met Daniel on her previous tour of duty in Medwich. Nothing would surprise her about his habits.

'Also,' Spruce went on, 'the laundrette is very near the perimeter fence.' He stopped. 'It's odd how one starts talking or thinking of Bolly's in prison terms.'

Theodora nodded. 'Have you noticed how every bit of

helpfully jolly information is combined with an accompanying threat? "Here's your key. We'll fine you if you lose it." "Here's the theatre, you can't get in without your resident's pass" type thing.'

'Oh, yes, they're control freaks all right,' Spruce agreed.

'I'd have thought as a policeman you might rather have approved of keeping people in line.' She knew even as she spoke that she was not being fair to him.

'Rules are for villains. Treating everyone as though they were or would be one if you gave them half a chance simply makes more of them. And here, of course, you're paying them to bully you as part of your holiday.'

The heavy car spun through the sparse out-of-season, out-of-town traffic. They moved fast along the closed esplanade of Highcliffe. Its booths and pavilions were shuttered. The sea smelled salty. Far out the lights of a passing boat looked more welcoming than the resort.

'I'd hate to make a connection between the Church and the persecuted holiday-maker,' Theodora murmured. But she knew Spruce would not be able to respond to that. His thoughts were utterly concentrated on the case. 'So why put him in a washing machine? Why not just leave him in the laundrette?'

'If they were disturbed, it might have been all that was to hand. As I say, if they intended getting him off site it was near the fence. Also laundrettes are kept open all hours.'

'Never locked?'

'People like your Daniel, do washing when they haven't anything better to do. And, an unwonted generosity on the management's part' – Spruce grinned – 'out of season they keep it unlocked so that their own people can use its facilities as well. Provided, of course, they don't get in the way of the visitors.'

'How did you learn that?'

'The boy manager, Victor. Well, he's not a boy, he's

twenty-six, but they all look like boys to me nowadays. Sign of an ageing policeman.'

'And does Victor make use of it?'

'Yes, and so does his cook, Tibor Maciewicz, and a couple of kitchen girls, Italians.'

'I suppose they have difficulty recruiting staff here. Did any of them see anything last night?'

'The Italians and Tibor were fully occupied in the kitchen until after the end of supper at nine. He said in his statement, as far as I can remember, "I do it midnight sometimes after a shift but I no got time last night." The two Italian girls are never out of each other's company and they swore they hadn't a minute to leave the kitchen and Tibor seems to bear that out.'

'So if anyone was seen going in, it wouldn't have looked unusual and it was kept unlocked. What was he wearing,' Theodora asked, 'this jester priest, when he was killed?'

'He wasn't wearing clerical dress. He'd got grey slacks and a running top – blue thin cotton.'

'It was a wet cold night.'

'Quite,' said Spruce, was well in step with her. 'We're looking for the anorak or coat or whatever because the running top was quite dry.'

'And when did he arrive on site?'

'He came down, or anyway he registered early. Mr Teane ticked him off his list in Warm Welcome at about ten-thirty in the morning and gave him his chalet key and so on.'

'What did he do between ten-thirty and his death?'

'We're working on it. It's difficult. Not many people knew him and filling up for a conference people don't notice strangers in a terrain where everybody is a stranger.'

'Have you looked through his things?'

'In the chalet? Yes. A single nylon bag, shaving stuff and a clown's costume.'

'Nothing to read?'

'Prayer book. Bible. But, and this must be significant, a wallet with a tenner in it and nothing else whatsoever. No driving licence, no credit cards, no old bills.'

'He travelled light.'

'Or didn't want his life traced, which?'

'We don't know enough to say,' Theodora objected.

'Nope.' Spruce ran his gloved hand down the steering wheel. Theodora recognised tension.

'Where does he live, I mean when he's not in a chalet at Bolly's?'

'That's another difficulty. He has no bank account and no permanent address as far as we can ascertain.'

'It's not enough, is it?'

'Not by a long chalk,' the Superintendent agreed.

They had begun to climb the slight hill inland which would lead them to the coast road to Felixstowe. As they shot past the turning, Theodora caught a glimpse of the signpost to Wrackheath, two miles. She thought of her cousin and his son but then put her own troubles aside and turned back to Spruce. She was surprised by how much he had been willing to share with her. Was it a sign of how much the case worried him? He'd dealt with the Church before. Behind apparent openness there would be many who would have as their first priority the concealing of anything which could bring the Church into disrepute.

'The last time we . . .' Spruce began hesitantly.

Theodora nodded. Their last co-operation, so successful in many ways, so painful in others, had been in the adjacent diocese of Norwich about ten years ago.

'On that occasion the Reverend Hereward Marr got his neck broken in his own church for beating up his wife.'

'A layman killed him. That I can understand. But what if a priest killed a priest?'

'It's unheard of. It's unimaginable,' Theodora said. The brotherhood matters. They'll support each other against any outside enemy, any layman, right or wrong. I never know whether to admire it or not.'

'We all do it,' said Spruce. 'The force is just the same. Even bad apples.'

'I wonder why I don't feel like that?'

'Don't you? No, I see you don't.'

'What am I missing?'

'Comfort. Strength in numbers. Acceptance. Where do you go for those?'

'Prayer,' Theodora answered. 'Sacrament, reflection on Scripture. All the things invented by the brotherhood, in fact.'

'Makepeace was a loner,' Spruce said softly. 'You ought to be able to understand him.'

Theodora chose not to reply. 'When was he killed?'

'He was killed between six-thirty and seven on Monday evening. We've still to complete the cross-checking, of course but it does look as though the number of people who could have been in that area was enormous and most were clergy. The laity are fewer in number and mostly have alibis. Supper was at eight, a bit later than normal to allow for late arrivals checking in. But frankly there seem to have been a dozen or more who could have been there if they'd wished.'

'Do any of them admit to having been in the area?'

'Not one. Most hadn't found their way about the place. Or can't have known if they had passed it. I think many of them were still coping with the cultural shock of the accommodation. In fact, to get to the chalets you'd have no reason to go round by the laundrette – unless you were lost.'

'What about someone looking for the chapel?'

'Yes, I'd thought of that. It's odd, that chapel. It's very small for a start. I gather it's consecrated by the RCs for the use of a priest who comes in to chaplain RC Bolly Holidayers during the season. Out of season it isn't used.

So your lot didn't intend to use it originally. It's not on the plan given to the conference-goers.'

'Well, it's too small for most of our purposes. It can't hold more than twenty or so.'

'Nevertheless, some of your people are or were intending to use it. I gather they've made an arrangement with Father O'Connor for the duration of the conference.'

'Forward in Faith, the Catholic wing of the Anglican Church, who oppose the ordination of women,' said Theodora to enlighten Spruce. Then she thought of Canon Oldsalmon and Father Sentinel. 'Is it important?'

'It might be,' Spruce admitted. 'You see there's a door between the laundrette and the chapel.'

'Why?'

'Fire regs.'

'Was anyone using the chapel at the time the body was put next door?'

'We haven't found anyone yet.'

'So really the leads from the scene of crime are not all you could wish.'

'You could say that.'

'Much, therefore, will depend on what we can find out about Joshua, his own personality, his friends, his background. It comes down to motive, doesn't it?'

'Who would want to kill a blameless priest?'

CHAPTER FIVE

Curriculum Vitae

'Twenty minutes,' said Spruce as they reached the by-pass and increased speed. They began to tick off the villages. Theodora remembered them as a litany from her youth. Strawborough, Mousebeech, Hodsleigh, Wrattingthorpe. In the sporadic lights of the main streets they looked much as they had in her youth. The brick and flint terraces hadn't been gentrified; they were too far from London and the railway service was awful.

'So, what's the local crime like?' Theodora gave Spruce a chance to range over his subject.

'The port expansion's made a difference. Diversified our trade with our European partners and all that.' Spruce rose to the prompt. 'Ports mean drugs and other sorts of goodies going round the side of customs. It's brought jobs, of course. But sailors drink an awful lot so there's more violence. Still, it's not the Met, and murder, apart from the odd domestic out in the sticks, is still uncommon.'

The lights of the port came up on the driver's side. Then in another ten minutes they'd left it behind and were once more in estuary country. Theodora thought how much she liked the meeting of sea and land, how such terrain retained its nature and history in the face of all that modern life could do to it. It was defended by the secret penetration of sea into its many inlets. Twice in the diurnal round land was transformed into marsh. She wound down the window and let the cold wet air into the speeding car. Now in the darkness she could feel the changes and smell the mixed scent of salt and diesel.

Another ten minutes and Spruce drew the car into a lay-by, switched on the light and consulted a four-inch-to-the-mile Ordnance Survey map.

'Braden Loke, past the Anchor in Hope on our right hand and over the drain.'

'Shall I navigate?' Theodora volunteered.

He handed her the map and they started off. They crossed a railway line of the sort that has gates which have to be opened and closed. It took the speed and hence the urgency out of the journey. It gave a feeling of entering a guarded and fenced land, an island where, perhaps, different laws and customs obtained. The sound of the tyres changed as they hit the potholes of the track. The headlights picked out stunted, leafless hedgerows rising above deep ditches. Theodora felt herself slipping back to childhood when exploring such lanes had been a deep pleasure, a relief indeed from the demands of social life with the family. She remembered how then they had seemed tenanted by people from another age, speaking another tongue. Had this been the country of Joshua's childhood too? And had he relished it or hated it? The cold air smelled of weed and rotting wood.

They swung round a sharp bend and there, surprisingly, was a freshly painted white wooden gate with a couple of small figures crouched on top of the posts. In the light of the headlamps, Theodora could make out a pair of plastic dwarves clutching fishing rods. She worked the latch, avoiding their scowling, humorous gaze. The Rover edged forward through a yard filled with bits of boats. Between the hulks of beached yachts raised on chocks could be seen rose bushes confined into odd bits of space, survivors from an earlier use of the property.

The car lurched to a halt close to the door of the timber and brick structure of the house. Spruce squeezed out and edged between the car and the building. He looked for a bell. It was mounted on a wooden beam, the clapper attached to a rope. The sound rang round the house. They were standing, Theodora realised, on a duckboard which squelched into the mud beneath. When the February floods came, she guessed the barn-like structure would more or less float. At the sound of the bell came two sharp barks and then a lot of growling. Finally, after much drawing of chains and sliding of bolts, the door was opened a foot and a face not unlike the gnomes on the gateposts peered up at them. Three feet below the master's face appeared the dog's; an old intelligent Alsatian gave them the once-over.

'Captain Makepeace? I'm Superintendent Spruce, Medwich CID, and this is the Reverend Theodora Braithwaite.' Spruce was punctilious.

The old man must have been in his late seventies. He was dressed in a dark green pullover and the sort of cord breeches with laces down the calf which are extremely difficult to purchase nowadays. He spoke no word but beckoned them inside. He cleared his throat at the dog who moved grudgingly aside and pushed his nose warningly into the back of Spruce's knees. They followed him along a narrow passage which opened out into a hall and staircase and then into a room, half study, half workshop. The shelves near the door were book filled, those near the large French window had tools, models of ships, clamps and rolled-up tubes of drawings. There was no desk but a table cum workbench at the far end did instead. In the grate a coke fire burned, giving a parsimonious heat into the dusty air.

In front of it were a sofa and a easy chair in ancient red hide which Theodora knew before she tried it would immediately sink into the floor. She and Spruce took the sofa, the old man the chair. The dog placed himself in front of the fire and settled down to follow the conversation.

The old man turned his face towards them. His head was round and his face reddish-orange like a fruit from an autumn tree. His hair was white and cut *en brosse*.

'I'm so very sorry about your son, about Joshua,' Theodora said, speaking she felt for both of them.

There was a pause. Theodora, who was used to dealing with grief, waited; she was prepared to do so all night if necessary. The old man nodded, acknowledging the propriety of her words. A sudden draught from the door ruffled his white hair and made it stand up like a hackle, giving him for a moment a fierceness, an indestructibility that came through in his voice.

'The Lord gives and the Lord has taken away. I can accept his loss if it is God's will. After all, many fathers have had greater losses. My own father had two sons killed in the war. I was too young and so survived.'

He turned his gaze on the Superintendent. 'What I do find hard to bear is the manner of his death.' The old man's tone was low and firm, the tones of a man who has worked amongst men for whose lives he was responsible. Theodora looked at the small neat head with its pointed jaw and the eyes, a pale bluish-grey found in so many sailors, as though their eyes were in some way related to the sea.

'I'm glad you've come,' he said suddenly. 'Both of you.' He turned from Spruce to Theodora. 'It makes me feel things are moving. In disaster there's always something that can be done. Or there isn't. In which case we must learn to sit still and not rock the boat. But here something can be done, can't it?'

'Yes,' said Spruce. 'You can be sure of that. We need to

know as much about your son as you can bear to tell us. At the moment we lack background. He seems to have led a private life.'

The old man sat still. His hand sought the head of his dog stretched out at his feet. He began rhythmically to stroke the long dark hair.

'Whatever you can tell us about your son may be of use. Until we know we can't tell,' Spruce prompted. Theodora thought, We're not small in our demands. In the midst of his grief we want him to sum up a life, a beloved life and do so in such a way as to reveal those features which might have led to his violent death.

The old man looked from one to the other. 'Where to start, eh? A sort of test of how well I knew Joshua. Well, I think I knew him pretty well. What I don't know so much about is the details of his existence. I mean his current life. Contacts, friends. We were close, you know. I thank God for that. Only sons and fathers, it's not always so. He felt what I felt. We didn't need to exchange trivia.'

'Tell us about him as a character,' Theodora prompted. 'What was he like in that way?'

'A good son, a good priest.' The old man was judicious, striving to be objective. 'He wasn't a career sailor but he did go into the service to please me. I always felt a man should know the elements of life. That's what the services teach you to know, the basic things, friends and God, safety and danger and how to arrange those things into a meaningful pattern. How hard these things are to get hold of . . . to balance the claims of . . .' The old man trailed off, then he regained his thread. 'And when he got in, I think he enjoyed it. He always made the best of things, even as a boy. To be honest, I think he was a bit too bright to make a career of it. He took after his mother in that respect, he got his brains and perhaps his wider interests from her.'

'Did he keep up with his friends from that time?' Spruce nudged him back to the point.

'I think some of them.'

'Can you give us any names?'

Makepeace thought for a moment. 'Martin, Martin Guard was an old shipmate. Much younger but service in the same ship binds men together.'

'And what did he do between 1976 and '78? Between leaving the service and going for ordination training?'

'Abroad. He went abroad with some missionary society to find out if he wanted to take orders.'

'Which one?'

'Not one I know much about. Fancy name. Adjumentum Salvatoris.'

'Where do they operate?'

'World wide. They have houses all over.'

'So where did Joshua go?'

The old man looked embarrassed. 'I never knew. I think he wanted to be away from us all for a bit. What is it you say?' He looked at Theodora. 'To test his vocation.'

'Didn't he keep in touch?'

'Oh yes, he contacted his friends in England and they had orders to ring me.'

'Was Martin Guard one of those?'

'Yes, he was, but there were others.'

'Who?' Spruce was urgent.

'It's no good. I don't remember. It's a long time ago. I know he wanted me to know he was well and I was grateful for that.' For a moment he looked desolate. 'What more had I a right to? What more could he have done?'

'When did you last see your son, Captain Makepeace?' Spruce was infinitely gentle.

'Sunday. He used to come over most Sunday evenings if he was in the area, after he'd done his evensong or whatever he was involved in. We'd have a bite together and so on.'

'And am I right in thinking your son had no settled abode?' Theodora thought, Well, Spruce has to use the jargon of his tribe sometimes.

'He once said to me, religious people must live as warriors.'

Spruce was lost. 'You mean always ready for a fight?'

'No, not quite like that. I think he meant in the fashion of some of the Eastern religions where it means we must be self-reliant, self-sufficient, not needing other people to serve us.'

Theodora understood him. 'In that way we are utterly free to serve others. We have no baggage. Some of the religious orders have that idea too. Franciscans.' She stopped then. She wondered if Adjumentum Salvatoris had something like that in their rule.

'My son had a cause,' the old man said. 'He used to say, "A man in orders is a man under orders."'

'And what was his cause?' Theodora put the question.

'I remember someone once asked him, "Whose side is God on?" He said, "On the side of the losers." And that was Josh's side.'

'How did it show itself?'

'He wouldn't climb ladders.'

Spruce looked baffled.

'He wouldn't see life in terms of achievement. He wouldn't go up the Church hierarchy. He gave up his parish, you know.'

Spruce nudged things back to a track he more readily understood. 'Where had he been before he came to you on Sunday?'

'He came up from Felixstowe. I think he'd been staying with some friends at the university.'

'And when you saw him on Sunday, did he seem to be all right then? I mean, was there anything on his mind, did you gather?'

'He was right as a rib stone pippin,' answered the old man and laughed. Then stopped.

'So he went on from here straight to Bolly's for the conference. What time did he leave here?'

'He was gone before I was up.'

'Which was?'

'About six, I suppose. I generally wake about then and take Bosun out.'

The dog, hearing his name, looked up intelligently.

'Was that what he usually did when he stayed here, I mean leave before you were awake?'

'Sometimes. It depended. But it wasn't unusual, if that's what you're asking.'

'And how often did he stay here?'

'When it was convenient to him. When he had work in this area. I tell you he was a warrior, a pilgrim.'

'About how often did that work out in practice?'

'Perhaps about once every six weeks. I think he wanted to keep an eye on me, see I was all right.'

'Did he have his mail sent here?' Spruce was being thorough, Theodora saw.

'No. Leastways, not usually.'

'But sometimes?'

'Yes.'

'Recently?'

The old man didn't reply for a minute. Theodora felt he was wondering how much to reveal. Then he said, 'The last couple of times he came, last month, mid-October that would be, and those times there was a letter waiting for him.'

'Did you happen to notice where from?' Spruce was delicate.

'Holland. Both times.' His tone was curt as though he regretted having to reveal something which had been given him in confidence.

'A letter, or a package, or what?'

'Brown A4 envelope. Single sheet. No sender's address.' Once he'd decided to give the information he clearly saw no reason not to be exact.

'And when he was not here, how did you keep in touch with your son?'

'Every now and again, perhaps once every ten days, he'd ring me from wherever he was.'

'And did he always tell you where he was?'

'Not unless it was of interest. If he thought I might know the place. If he were in Bristol or Southampton or Liverpool he'd know I'd know the country, the port, and we'd have a chat.'

'Do you know what sort of places Joshua usually stayed at?'

'He had friends all over.'

'And if there were no friends?'

'The clergy are hospitable, at least the parish clergy are. Or so Josh used to say. And then again, if he were in a port, there's always the sailors' rest.'

'The Mission to Seamen,' Theodora interpreted.

'A good institution,' Captain Makepeace agreed. 'Keeps men out of the brothels.'

Theodora turned the subject. 'What made him take to clowning?'

'I told you, he had a mission. He wanted to help people to see the world differently. He thought it was easy to get stuck in our own safe habits. He once said we wrap our blankets round ourselves and snuggle into our hammocks and woe betide anyone who tries to shake us awake. Joking, jesting was a way of jolting people out of their ruts.'

'Did you yourself see him perform ever?'

'A few times.' The old man's face broke into a smile. 'He was clever. He was never a performer in his own right, always a comment on other people's performance. I've got some videos,' he said suddenly. 'Do you want to see them?'

The old man got up stiffly and went to the door. The dog faced a dilemma but in the end, in a stiff mimic of his master's walk, he tapped his way across the bare boards of the room and followed him out.

Spruce looked at Theodora. 'I wonder if he suspects anyone?'

Theodora shook her head. 'Martin Guard is the only name that has come up. Do you think he knows Guard is at the conference?'

From upstairs came the sound of opening drawers and after a moment the dog came padding back. The coke in the grate creaked as it collapsed into itself. Beyond that there was no sound. Theodora thought, This is the pace he lives at and these are the sounds he hears, the sounds of the natural not the social world.

Captain Makepeace pushed a plastic carrier on to the table and sat down again. 'I don't have a TV or a video or a projector but Joshua wanted me to have them. I think he felt it was a bit like copies of the books you write or the money you put in the bank. Safe as houses here.'

'Didn't Joshua feel he was safe then?' Spruce asked.

'Dangerous world out there.'

'But specifically? Was there anyone or anything you know of which might have threatened your son's life?'

'He helped people, all sorts. Didn't count the cost. Bound to make you enemies.'

'When?'

'Always, but particularly when he was in that chaplaincy at Felixstowe. He did three years there.'

'But' – Spruce attempted to nail this elusive old man – 'you can't think of anyone who would want to kill your son or who would have a reason to do so?'

The old man looked away from them. 'Amazing what people will kill for,' was as far as he would go.

★ ★ ★

'So,' said Spruce as they hit the main road after the bumps of the track and began to pick up speed. 'Where did that get us?'

Theodora picked her words carefully. 'I think he may know or suspect but won't say.'

'Person or motive?'

'That's the same in this case, isn't it?'

'So why isn't he telling?' Spruce's way of showing frustration was to move his hand up and down the wheel. 'Is it fear?'

'I get the impression not much frightens that old man.'

'Well, what then?'

'He's a man of faith,' Theodora ventured. She was never too sure how far Spruce would follow arguments of that kind. His curiosity for new ideas, new people, new emotions even, she did not doubt. But was that fuel enough to enable him to follow what were, when she produced them in the light of day, flimsy intuitions about how such elements worked in the psychology of those who had religious convictions. 'He would be scrupulous about casting doubt without proof. He might even hold some sort of notion that all is in the hands of God and that in His own good time He would work things out.'

'He seemed eager enough to set things going when we first started talking to him,' Spruce said.

'So if he changed his mind in the course of our questioning it might be because things suddenly got clearer for him.'

'Can you pin down when that point might have been reached?' Spruce spared her a glance.

'It was when we got to that eighteen-month absence from home when Joshua was keeping in contact by getting his friends to ring him from abroad.'

'So we need to fill in the time scale.'

'Might we be able to do that through Martin Guard?'

'He's certainly someone I'll have to see again.'

Theodora noticed the pronouns. She was allowed to help with the comforting of bereaved parents but had no place in the official questioning of what might be key witnesses, might even turn out to be murderers. She quite understood. She had no wish to intrude. If Spruce thought it appropriate he'd let her know the outcome.

'What about the videos?' Theodora pressed. 'Why did he store them with his father who couldn't ever play them back?'

'I hope we might find that out when *we* play them back.'

'When? Tonight?'

'I think I'd rather look at them fresh. Could you manage nine o'clock tomorrow?'

Theodora was amused to see that she had been readmitted to the process. Perhaps if it were a matter of being funny about the Church, then Spruce might be diffident of his own ability to get the joke. Hence Theodora would be useful.

'I shall be at mass at seven-thirty but since Canon Oldsalmon's celebrating I shall be able to make nine and still get breakfast.'

'Good,' said Spruce and appeared to switch off thinking about the case, another reason perhaps for his success. 'Would you have time for a toasted cheese? The Buccaneer does quite a good one at this time of night.' He prodded towards the night outside the windscreen.

Theodora thought of the soggy quiche and mashed potatoes she'd pushed around her plate three hours ago. Toasted cheese seemed a cheerful idea. The pub's sign came suddenly out of the darkness as the car left the country and hit the lights of Highcliffe. Round the side there was a good crowd of cars indicating a popular house. A wave of noise, smoke and music met them as they pushed open the door of the clapboard building. Spruce was known so they were served at once.

'These country-town pubs are so different from the London ones,' Theodora said as she sliced the toast into quarters. 'Even though they serve the same beer.'

'How?' Spruce was busy amalgamating ketchup with mustard in a businesslike manner.

'Different accents, of course, but even the busy ones are less frenetic too. I suppose they've spent the day doing things more slowly, less stressful therefore.'

'Going to retire to the country, are you?' Spruce asked.

Theodora thought of her own melting pot on the bank of the Thames. 'No. Not yet. The buzz still excites me. But it's nice to come out occasionally, to know there is an alternative. Perhaps I'll retire to the country thirty years from now.'

'Won't be any by then.' Spruce wasn't jeremiading, just factual. 'South-east England will be one long concrete suburbia.'

'Then I shall go to the north and live in a cave on the moors.'

As they stepped once more into the night air there came the sound of raised voices from the far end of the car park. Theodora caught a glimpse of the faces, white against the shadows. There were three figures grouped round a dark blue Transit van, the driver's door of which was open. Spruce pulled up short and listened.

'You promised. You told me.' The accent wasn't quite right, Theodora thought. There was a gabble of further talk. Then two of the men got into the van and left the third on the verge as it drew away in a crash of gears.

As they got into the Rover Spruce remarked companionably, 'That was Nick Trimming and his friends, Jason Taint and Dave the Merc.'

* * *

Kenneth Bloomfield was saying, 'The Wittgensteinian position absolutely forbids that conclusion. Could I have the sugar?'

Three or four clerical faces registered courteous bafflement. It was early in the day for such heights, they felt as they toyed with Tibor's ideas of an English breakfast in the Splendide Diner.

Kenneth never brought his Christian faith under the scrutiny of his intellect. He had imbibed from his family the concepts of good pastoring, good fellowship and good teaching. In the latter he did not mean sound theology, indeed he tried to hear as little theological preaching as possible. He meant moral and social teaching. These traits he retained even after his conversion to philosophy.

From the springboard of a suburban comprehensive and A levels in Religious Education and British Constitution, Kenneth had read Theology as a first degree at Birmingham. There, one day, he had strayed into an open Philosophy of Language seminar. A couple of visiting Cambridge postgraduates had been in full flood. He experienced, he used to say, his 'Damascus road'. He'd been entranced. Their certainty, their careful ordering of the world into related parts, took his breath away. They used words like 'truth' and 'reality' and 'meaning' as though they knew what they meant and not just as particles to give emphasis to their own opinions, as was the practice of the lecturers he'd listened to in Theology. Their private conversation too, he realised when he sought out their company afterwards, was like a chess game. The moves of each in relation to the other could be foretold but not quite. They spoke of Plato as though they had read him. Their tones were of good-humoured scorn as they moved round the positions of other philosophers. Kenneth longed for that unchallengeable confidence, which the status of philosopher seemed to confer.

Moreover, he noticed as he cultivated their acquaintance, they never switched off. They never stopped philosophising. The most commonplace everyday activities, plunging hands into basins of hot water, looking down magnifying glasses, waking from dreams, were all occasions for launching into problems of knowledge, perception and epistemology.

They were in this respect religious. This suited Kenneth because he too was deeply religious. He had separated his intellectual pursuits from that deep, thirsty, religious simplicity which had brought his family from Judaism to Baptists in the second British generation. But his intellectual gifts never prevented his being regular at worship. He progressed from the certainties of the Christian Union of his school and university to the rather different certainties of Anglo-Catholicism in his local parish church in Felixstowe. His love affair with philosophy was of the head but it could not undermine his religious heart.

When Kenneth had drunk of the philosophic spring, when he'd listened to his Cambridge philosophers, he wanted to be one of them. He saw his tutor and changed his course. He emerged two years later with a first in part one theology and a first in part two philosophy. He was a most finished product of the subject. He proceeded without difficulty to doctoral research at UEA. He havered between Aesthetics and Philosophy of Religion. When it came down to, he was wont to say, was, did you enjoy puncturing the woolly, unexamined generalisations of the artistically pretentious (see any art gallery catalogue), or the unanalysed metaphysical nonsense of theologians (see Teilhard de Chardin). In the end he went for the theologians' throats.

His pilgrimage from Judaeo-Baptist to Anglo-Catholicism had provided him with release and freedom. He could, he had the right to, tell other people what to think and indeed what thinking was. He was cleverer than his great-grandfather who had been a rabbi in Poland. He was a great deal more intellectually secure than his father who had sold musical instruments in Huddersfield. He had spotted a niche market which he reckoned would carry him through a professional career. Philosophy of Religion was, as they said, an undeveloped area.

He had written his thesis on 'A Critique of the Hermeneutical Presuppositions of Twentieth-century Commentators on St John's Gospel in the Light of Postmodernist Understanding of Meta-narrative.' When a non-philosophical friend had suggested that this sounded like commentary on commentary, he'd been able to reply, 'No, commentary on commentary on commentary. Just what philosophy should be doing.'

It had been well received. On the strength of it he did a year lecturing at a Midwestern university. It had provided him with the equivalent of a finishing school. They had been very kind and hospitable to him. They were quite used to listening to lecturers from universities they had never heard of. He'd enjoyed the American academic scene and adopted some of its manners, speech and dress habits. For an engagement at a conference such as this in late November he wore a green shirt with a round collar and a lightweight blue nylon suit.

At Bolly's Jolly Holiday Home this bright November morning, the prospect was fair. He was about to take, he hoped, a further step in his career. At forty-three it was time to shed the young Turk image. He was within striking distance of a chair. There had been moves to put one in with Church sponsorship at the new University of Felixstowe. There was still a fair amount of Christianity of the nonconformist sort in the Eastern counties. A frozen fruit millionaire with a Methodist background had offered money ('The mediaeval hunger to atone,' Kenneth had murmured) and the diocese of Medwich had been put in charge of the appointments' panel. This conference therefore was important to Kenneth. He needed to impress. There was a bishop present. There would be senior clergy and laity.

Theodora, on the same table at breakfast, watched him with interest. She'd read his book. It was thorough and scholarly. He made the right connections. In a way it was a very orthodox piece of philosophical writing. But (she applied her own criteria to it) how was the understanding of the Faith enhanced by it?

He felt her eye on him and leaned across the table to get a better view of her name label, slightly curling on this the second day of the conference but bravely attached to her chest. There was a moment of double take.

'Theodora Braithwaite. Have I met you someplace before?'

'I don't think I've had that pleasure.' Theodora was prepared to be agreeable.

'Here, wait a minute, did I read you in *CHR* on . . . who was it?'

'Thomas Henry Newcome, nineteenth-century Tractarian, founder of the Order of St Sylvester and indeed much else,' supplied Canon Oldsalmon, who kept up a modest programme of scholarly reading which included the works of old friends.

Kenneth calculated quickly. 'Right, thought I remembered it.' That didn't after all commit him to much.

'It's a very good article,' said Canon Oldsalmon, quick to defend his friends.

Kenneth needed to know more before spending time and energy. 'Is there a book in there somewhere?' He smiled, the older scholar to the younger one.

'In the spring,' Theodora admitted.

'Who's doing it?'

'OUP,' said Theodora and knew she'd won on that one.

'Hey, you and me must have a mardle,' Kenneth admitted checkmate. The area of scholarship was deeply unfashionable but the publisher the best. Who was this too tall woman with the too conventional manner? Was she or was she not worth cultivating? Better take no chances. It's easier to drop than to try and take up the slighted. 'Are you doing something here?'

Theodora nodded. 'I've got a slot on the last day.'

'On?'

'Women's ministry.'

Kenneth knew how to assess that one. Women were no longer the coming bandwagon. They'd made it. People were tired of it. They'd moved on to homosexuality.

'A time for consolidation.'

'I imagine it's always a time for that.'

Theodora will be arguing for women not to seek priestly orders,' Canon Oldsalmon remarked with relish.

'Oh, right,' Kenneth had her taped now. She was some sort of masochistic nutcase. He almost physically brushed her off. 'Could I have some toast please?' His tone suggested someone might refuse him this modest request.

Theodora, however, reckoned she'd done her bit, provided some entertainment and she was owed. The table began to empty. Kenneth and she were alone at one end.

'Have you been at Felixstowe long?'

It was a light inquiry. She might just have been making conversation, smoothing over any previous roughness.

'Ten years.' He realised as he said it that that was much too long for a respectable young high-flyer. He should have gone someplace by now.

If Theodora thought this she gave no indication of it. Instead she went on, 'It has a very agreeable site and you were lucky to have St James on your boundaries to act as a chaplaincy.'

Kenneth agreed with all this.

'Did you by any chance know Joshua Makepeace? Or was he before your time?'

There was a moment's hesitation. 'Yes, I was very sorry to hear . . . I knew him when he was in his last year as chaplain there and I'd just got my tutorial fellowship.'

'Was he clowning when you knew him?'

'He always had that kind of physical approach to proclaiming the gospel. He'd mime things and use musical instruments to make points when he was preaching.' Kenneth's usually intense and concentrated expression relaxed into a genuine smile. 'He was great.'

'Why did he leave?'

'He said he wanted to move about a bit, go freelance and extend his talents. We don't let clergy do that so much here but in the States it's not so strange for a man to carve out his own ministry for himself and then to . . .' He trailed off.

Theodora followed his eye. On the far table was a copy of *The Times* propped in front of a figure. The Reverend Martin Guard was immersed in the headlines.

'Do you know Father Guard?' Theodora inquired.

'No,' said Kenneth firmly. 'No, I don't know him.'

CHAPTER SIX

Weapons of Death

'Have you decided for Jesus?'

'Not yet,' said Victor cautiously. He had no wish to offend a client but felt there were services which were beyond the call of duty. He looked at his watch for the third time in ten minutes. It read half past ten. 'I've got to do lunch, probably. Tibor's not turned up.'

Chris Teane gazed seriously into Victor's eyes in the harsh light of the kitchen. The place smelled of boiling water and disinfectant. Polished steel surfaces empty of human hands, empty of food, stretched as far as the eye could see. 'There are some things which are just too important to be put off,' he said firmly.

Victor's life was one of constant negotiation. Managers, he had been taught, have to compromise, reason, get consensus. He searched around in his armoury of techniques to see if he could find something to fit this one. 'I will think about it. I really will, but I don't know that much about . . .' He hesitated; it seemed somehow disrespectful to mention the name when he'd just said he didn't know him, 'Jesus.'

'I could help you to know Him.' Chris was ever so gentle.

'Why not come along to our young persons' group tonight in Red River Café, eight-thirty this evening?'

Victor gazed at his tormentor. He wanted to say, If you lot don't get lunch, adequate and on time in two and a half hours, I may not be in post by eight-thirty this evening. What business was it anyway of this old guy what his leisure-time pursuits were? Chris, who kept middle age at bay with an earring and who was fond of saying that the problem of our time for young people was how to spend an increasing amount of leisure, would have been unhappy to have penetrated Victor's thoughts.

'One or two very nice girls. Lots of fellowship,' he enticed.

'I've got a steady,' Victor said with dignity, though not entirely truthfully. He actually cringed at this brawny, short-sleeved, nylon-shirted, middle-aged bloke with his wide leather belt holding up designer jeans. 'Look, if you can give me a hand with this lot, I'll see what I can do about your prayer meeting or whatever this evening.'

Chris too was a negotiator and persistent. 'Okey dokey,' he said amenably. 'Where do you want me to start?'

Victor pushed a menu into his hand torn from the noticeboard beside the door. 'It's toad in the hole, French fries and cauliflower *or* lamb stew and beans; rice pudding *or* black forest gâteau.' He ticked off the origin of each of these goodies on his fingers. 'Stew needs decanting from the fridge.' He waved towards the cool room. 'The girls do the fries nearer the time. They're half cooked and defrosting over there.' He nodded to two huge vats in which, peeping from the top, Chris could see naked-looking white sticks which might once have belonged to a potato. 'Black forest and rice are individuals. Don't need anything doing. It's really just get the toad in the hole together and I'll do the cauli. The freezer does the rest.'

'Why don't you have frozen individual toads in holes?' Chris asked, curious.

Victor was shocked. 'We pride ourselves at Bolly's on the home-cooking touch,' he said with dignity. 'You'll need the sausages . . .'

'From the cool room,' Chris agreed. 'What time do the girls come in?'

'At the last minute,' said Victor bitterly. 'They know Tibor's little ways. I once had Ginetta and her niece doing the whole lunch for three hundred lawn-mower salesmen in under an hour. Boy, can those guys eat.'

'A challenge,' Chris agreed. 'Does Tibor often go awol?'

'Only if it would cause real difficulty,' Victor admitted.

'Has he . . .' Chris paused out of delicacy, 'a drink problem?'

'I don't think so. He's a hypochondriac. He spends hours and hours up the doctor's surgery or down in casualty.'

'Poor fellow. What's wrong with him?'

'He has boils,' said Victor with distaste. He really did try to be fair but he didn't like the contiguity of boils and food. It went against everything he'd learned on his NVQ in Catering Studies course.

'We have healing services at my church.' Chris never missed a trick. 'We have laying on of hands and exorcism. We think the healing ministry is very, very important in the modern world. You know, science misses out a lot of things.'

Victor didn't doubt it. But right now he had his priorities. 'Look, Chris, this is really, really kind of you but I've got to get on. The art of cookery' – his voice took on the more open vowels of his last cookery teacher who had come from Manchester – 'is all in the synchronisation of the defrosting. Too early or too fast and it all goes soggy, too late and you break your teeth. Everything depends on timing. Which is why Tibor is such a pain in the—'

'Right,' said Chris briskly. He'd come through the entire gamut of Church-related youth groups – Badgers, Beavers, Pathfinders, Young Pilgrims – and they'd all inculcated the same message: 'Lend a hand'. 'So it's the cold room first.'

'Right.'

'Where?'

'Behind the cookers, to your right.'

'It's locked.'

'Key's hung on the back of the door.'

'Why do you keep it locked?'

'Lot of valuable food in there. They're not above nicking the odd vacuum pack of bacon.'

Chris decided not to ask why, if that were so, the key was accessible to all and sundry. The big door – it was two foot taller than Chris who was five ten – swung open with that softness imparted by insulating materials. There was a large dark area inside with shelves running off at right angles in the manner of ample old pantries. 'Should there be a light?'

'Yes, there should.' Victor was brusque. There was a system, perfectly easy to work, for getting replacement light bulbs. You filled in, in triplicate, a pink slip, copies of which could be acquired from himself, and in due course he issued a replacement from stock. He'd explained it very carefully to Tibor when he first joined the staff. The trouble, as he well knew, was that Tibor's grasp of the language came and went in accordance with Tibor's interest in the subject. A man who could use words like 'haematologist' with complete correctness did not always gather the precise significance of 'a pink slip in triplicate'.

Chris went over to the cold-room door. He took his pencil torch from his pocket and played it round the shelves. 'There's the toads,' he said as it illuminated the rime-encrusted packages.

Chris moved towards them, then stopped and looked down at his feet. 'Does Tibor usually keep his clothes here?'

Victor felt this was really too much. He came up to Chris and looked down at the bundle on the tiled floor of the room. He stirred it with his foot and thought that this time

Tibor had gone too far. He'd have to put in for a replacement chef, whatever the inconvenience. He bent down and picked it up. Something metal clanged on to the tiles.

Chris clasped his arm. 'We'd better get that policeman,' he said and prevented Victor picking up the long knife wrapped in the leather jacket.

Theodora and Spruce had just got the screen arranged for the showing of Captain Makepeace's videos in Harries Bar when Victor banged on the door.

'It's the cold room, it's the knife,' he said with less than his usual organised aplomb.

Theodora saw no reason to absent herself from the development. Spruce and Tilby need not acknowledge her presence if they didn't feel like it. But she was curious to know what had come up. She might be six foot one and had, on occasion, a presence, yet she was remarkably self-effacing when she wanted to be. She followed the policemen and Victor across the road to the kitchens behind the Splendide Diner. Chris Teane had taken up a position like a security man at a club door. He stood with his back to the cold room with the door closed behind him. Spruce and Tilby went in.

After some minutes they re-emerged with the leather jacket in one plastic bag and a long black-handled knife in another. Spruce said, 'Can you identify the jacket?'

Victor nodded. 'It's Tibor's.'

'And where is Tibor now?'

'He left after breakfast about half after eight.'

'When was he supposed to return?'

'Ten. Certainly no later than half past.'

'Where did he go?'

'I really don't know, Superintendent.' Victor looked close to tears.

'Have you got his address?'

'In the office.'

'Right,' said Spruce. 'Can you get it for me?'

Victor nodded.

'And I'm afraid you'll have to close the kitchen for a couple of hours. We'll need to go over it.'

'But what about lunch? I mean they'll want their lunch.'

Theodora felt for him. A hundred and fifty hungry Anglicans fresh from a morning's intellectual debate and wanting to refuel was a daunting prospect.

Victor felt himself challenged as never before. 'I'll ring Fred, local chippie. Shop at the end of the alley, just outside the gate. See if I can do a deal with him.'

Theodora thought, That young man will go far.

'The post-modernist position, on the other hand . . .' Kenneth Bloomfield was holding forth from the platform. He had pushed his glasses off his nose and up his forehead so that he looked like a learned motor-cyclist. He had a loose-leaf manuscript propped on the lectern but he rarely needed to consult it. He commanded his subject. The clergy are not for the most part scholars. Many think they should be. Many pretended to be, but the standards are not what they were in their grandfathers' time. Archdeacon Treadwell in the front row slept.

In the body of the hall of The OK Corale Lucy Royal was not interested in the post-modernist position on St John's gospel. She did not feel she needed to advance her ideas beyond those clear and sustaining interpretations which she had been fed by Archdeacon Treadwell's father when he had prepared her for confirmation as a girl more than sixty-five years ago. St John for her was the universe brimful of light, chock-a-block with numinous power which illuminated the fundamental truth of love's victory over hate. Lucy's only problem, she felt, was how to align herself with the powers of light in the face of those of darkness in such a way as to let in the chinks of light to a Satanic world. The theory was less interesting than the practice. The theory was clear, if metaphorical. The practice, on the other hand, was a continuous confused warfare.

She had to admit to herself that she missed the struggles of the mission field where everything was a good deal plainer than it was here, what she still termed 'at home'. This terrible business of the young man (anyone under sixty was young to Lucy), the jester who had been killed and stuffed, apparently, into a washing machine. Then there was the question of those voices which, as she had told Canon Oldsalmon, she'd heard on her first night, plotting. Then there was this latest business. She'd told Arthur but Arthur was a very sound sleeper indeed. It had served him well in the discomforts of the bush but Lucy felt he ought to be a bit more alert now he was retired. She'd heard it quite clearly; the chug of an outboard above the splash of the tide on the beach. Then, and this is what she found so peculiar, the sounds of men conversing in Umundese.

Of course it wasn't a well-known African language. The country had less than a hundred thousand people in it all told. But she and Arthur had spent five happy years there. They'd got a health centre started and pushed for a primary school and with their own hands built a chapel. Together they had prayed and planned and taught. To hear that beautiful flexible African tongue coming clearly from the shores of the East Anglian coast was amazing. She'd got up and gone to the small doll's-house-sized window of the chalet and peered out into the thick darkness of the early hours of a November morning. When she'd told Arthur at breakfast-time he'd not been any help. 'My dear, I know you miss the work,' he'd said, treating her as though she were ill. 'I miss it too. But we did agree not to look back.'

'I wasn't dreaming,' she'd said. 'I am not so doddering

that I can't tell the difference between waking and dreaming.'

So now she sat in the Bloomfield key-note lecture on Wednesday morning and tried to work out what it all meant and what she should do. If there were Umundese visitors in Highcliffe, she ought to look them up. They were almost bound to have friends in common, the country being so small, the educated classes so tightly knit and the tribal system being what it was. And Umundese visitors might be lonely and in need of things which she could provide. Lucy's heart went out to them. Finally and most urgently to Lucy, if there were an organisation able and rich enough to provide for refugees, she could make use of their services for some of her own needy cases.

Up at the front Kenneth was getting technical about the difference between 'parole' and 'langue'. Lucy wondered which of these two St John had used in his writing and whether he knew which he was using and what were the advantages of the one over the other from the point of view of communicating the Truth. A row or two in front of her she could see the dark hair of Theodora who had come in a bit late and chosen the end of a row.

Lucy reached stiffly under her chair and recovered her handbag which was large and suitcase-like. She and Arthur both believed in carrying what you needed with you rather than trusting bearers. She scrabbled inside and found a neat leather-bound notebook with a small pencil attached. The world is divided into those who have mechanisms about them that work and the rest who don't. Lucy associated this difference with the one made by Our Lord between the wise and foolish virgins. Lucy was in the company of the wise. Her pencils never ran out of lead. Her torch had batteries in it. She had once heard primary-school children she was visiting in her last posting sing the song 'Give me oil in my lamp, keep me burning, keep me burning till the break of day'. Lucy had thought how apposite that was. She didn't usually like the modern choruses which were replacing the hymns of her youth with their splendidly rich theological content and lugubrious tramping tunes, but that one had a point, she felt.

She wrote in her careful copperplate on the lined paper. It took her some time because she had quite a lot to say. When, however, it was finished she folded it and tapped Arthur sharply on the arm. Her husband shuddered and came to life. He looked kindly on his wife and murmured, 'Eh?'

'To Theodora,' said Lucy, nodding her head in the direction of her correspondent. Arthur took the note and was about to pass it to his neighbour. He mimed writing the name on the note. Lucy looked at him in puzzlement. 'What?'

'Who to?'

'I told you, Theodora down there.'

'Put her name on the front,' Arthur suggested.

'Oh, yes, what a good idea.'

By this time there was a certain amount of turning round and clearing of throats in the Anglican fashion. Few might have been able to understand the business of the day from the platform but they all knew how to behave in an academic lecture.

Theodora was amongst those who were not giving their full attention to the intellectual content of the speech. She was occupied with reviewing the events of the last hour. She'd gone to keep her appointment with Spruce at eight-thirty in Harries Bar. There they'd been running late. The woman PC who knew how to merge and match in the computer records had come up with some information about where everyone was at the probable time of the killing according to their own statements cross-checked with those of others.

It was an important moment. Theodora realised that this was probably the moment when cases begin to make sense to those who are responsible for them and that the computer was actually a tool which made that cross-checking process much faster than having a man work through each statement by hand and eye. She realised too that Spruce probably ought not to have had her there when he and Tilby did the analysis. But he made no attempt to ask her to withdraw so she stayed.

Spruce ticked them off on his fingers. 'Between six-thirty and seven p.m. we have: one, Oldsalmon on his way from his chalet to take up his favourite armchair in Warm Welcome. Two, Father Martin Guard, bringing his luggage up from his car which, for some reason that we don't yet know, he'd chosen to leave on the quay. Three, Jason about to go on duty, on his way to the hut at the entrance barrier. And finally, and according to the Italian girls, who have had time to have second thoughts, damn them, Tibor was absent from the kitchen at that time, but we don't know he was actually in the area of the laundrette.'

Tilby asked, 'Do we know if any of them knew the victim?' He turned unexpectedly to Theodora. 'Would you know of any link between the priests for example and Joshua Makepeace?'

Theodora thought. 'Martin Guard and Canon Oldsalmon are linked by churchmanship. They both know each other as Anglo-Catholics. As far as I know that is Oldsalmon's only connection with Joshua. But we know Martin Guard knew him. He told me he served on the *Prometheus* with him and Captain Makepeace told Superintendent Spruce and me that Martin was one of the people who used to ring him when Joshua was out of the country.'

'It's not a lot to go on,' Spruce grumbled.

'Did all the information about where these four were

come from their own lips or are they all inferences from the cross-checking?'

'Canon Oldsalmon made no bones about saying he thought he had passed the laundrette on his way to Warm Welcome. He'd followed a sign which said 'chapel' but didn't realise when he saw it that it was next door to a laundrette. He says he saw Martin Guard carrying his luggage past the laundrette. Jason was seen by . . .' Spruce ran his Biro down the list, 'Martin Guard. And when we had another go at Guard he agreed that he *had* been in the area, entering at about a quarter to seven and as he rounded the corner to go past Warm Welcome to his chalet, he saw Jason coming past at a run in the direction of the entrance.'

'Have you questioned Jason?'

'He's off duty until this afternoon. We'll have another go at him then.'

'Did he lie in his first statement or what?'

Tilby thought, She's quite good at this game for an untrained mind. Spruce flicked the roll of computer paper and looked down. 'He says here, "I was on the barrier from four-thirty to seven-thirty. I didn't see no one strange coming except them coming in for the conference. I didn't see no one going out neither." We'll have to have another word with Jason since he doesn't mention being absent from his post at the critical time.'

'And what about Tibor?' Theodora pursued.

'As I say, we don't know he was in the area at the time. We only know that between six-forty-five and seven he wasn't in the kitchen. Both the Italian girls agree on this because it's a bad time for him to be absent. They're coming up to taking things from ovens and putting them into containers ready for serving.'

'Does he often go out at this time?' In her time as an undergraduate Theodora had worked in kitchens. She knew the habits of chefs. There was a generally predictable pattern to their behaviour: those who smoked needed to have a drag after the strains of preparation and before the serving.

Spruce knew what she meant. 'We'll need to check that with the Italians and also with Victor the manager.'

It was at that point that Victor brought news from the kitchen. All thought of the videos had to be abandoned.

Theodora felt she ought to try to attend to what Kenneth Bloomfield was saying even though right now she was less interested in the reinterpretation of St John than in how Joshua Makepeace had met his death and why. She had begun to make some headway into the jargon of Kenneth's thesis when she felt a tap on her shoulder. In her present abstracted state she jumped as though she had been stabbed and fumbled the note which was pushed into her hand. She read:

Dear Theo, I hate to trouble you but do you happen to know any Umundese? I seem to remember you did a stretch in Nigeria and travelled north into that interesting country. And I thought you said you once met Mr Ngaio, a very dear man (did you know he had been made Archdeacon?). Well, if you do I think there are some in Highcliffe. I heard them talking last night. Don't you think that we ought to try and find out where they are and make contact? I should think they might be very lonely in East Anglia in this weather so very different from their own climes. And secondly, I think we ought to have a word about the Bishop's peep show yesterday. I have an idea that it might be a plot on the part of AS. Do you know them?

Theodora considered all this. Of course Lucy Royal was a great dear but she must be in her eighties now. Was her mind failing? On the other hand, Lucy might be quite sane but just bored with the lecture and wishing therefore to keep herself awake by gossiping with an old friend. There was nothing fanciful with the content. Lucy was quite right that she had been in Nigeria for part of her first curacy. She did know Umundi. She had met the Reverend, now Archdeacon, Isaiah Ngaio. How very apt! Now she came to think of it he had apprentice Archdeacon written all over him when she met him as a student while he was at Gracemount three years ago. That his rise had been rapid might well be due to the uncertain conditions of a country where disease and sudden death were commonplace, not to mention martyrdom. For there, both paganism and Islam were rivals to Christian truth. It was not inconceivable too that Lucy had indeed heard the Umundese language in Highcliffe. If it seemed unlikely, it wasn't actually mad.

It was when she got to the last line that she wondered if Lucy might not be wandering a bit. Did she really know something about the cause of the confusion at the Bishop's lecture? And what was the reference to AS? Theodora ran through the possible meanings of the initials. Army service corps – hardly. Auxillary Semtex. She looked vaguely round her. There at the far end was Father Martin Guard. Adjumentum Salvatoris. 'The Upholders of the Saviour'. Was that what Lucy meant? But surely that rather surreptitious missionary society wouldn't concern itself with wrecking the Bishop's great moment. Admittedly the society was not supportive of evangelical bishops but it would still be a childish thing to do. Theodora turned the name over in her mind. Where had she heard it recently? Then she remembered Captain Makepeace had said it was with that society that Joshua had enrolled for a couple of years when testing his vocation. Did Lucy know that? Did she indeed know Joshua the jester? She hadn't mentioned the murder, only the Bishop's mishap. She had better have a word with Lucy at the coffee break. She looked at the blue fluorescent hands of the clock behind the speaker's head. Ten minutes to coffee break. Then fifteen minutes for coffee. Then, presumably, Kenneth would take questions.

Theodora twisted round in her seat, sought out Lucy and mimed drinking. Lucy nodded purposefully with immediate comprehension. So that was fixed. How, she wondered, was Spruce getting on in the kitchen quarters?

Spruce spread the coat out gently on the table in Harries Bar. The knife had been dispatched by car to the forensic laboratory in Medwich. It would be five hours before anything came back. He'd send the coat too in due course but Spruce liked to look at things before forensic got their people on it. Sometimes it saved days of work.

Spruce drew on a pair of plastic gloves in a gesture which looked like that of a surgeon and spread the coat out carefully on the stained bar table. It looked forlorn, dead almost. For a moment it occurred to Tilby to wonder if its owner was indeed still alive.

'The anatomy lesson. Twenty-first century style,' said Spruce to disguise his feelings. Then he began his commentary while Tilby wrote it all down.

'Leather well worn, brown, three sets of two buttons, epaulettes also buttoned. Fleece lined' – Spruce opened the coat out further – 'also very well worn. Leather collar. Two pockets at hand level outside and one pocket at breast level inside.' Spruce raised his head. 'Do you get the impression this wasn't made in England?'

'Maker's tab?' Tilby asked.

Spruce ran his finger round the collar seam. There was nothing. Then he tracked down through the fleece towards the inside pocket where one might expect it. He bent his head and pulled the pile of the fleece apart. 'It's been cut out. Look.' He offered his find to Tilby. 'It looks quite deliberate, not wear and tear but someone wanting to make sure this couldn't be traced.'

Tilby made his note and Spruce went on to the pockets. 'Contents?' Tilby allowed himself a note of eagerness.

Spruce inserted his hands into each in turn. In the right hand outside pocket he extracted a wallet and a crumpled handkerchief. The two men brought their heads together over the item. It too had a well-used look. Very carefully Spruce opened it up. There were two ten-pound notes in the right hand flap and in the left a National Health card and a doctor's prescription.

'No credit cards?'

'No.'

Spruce was about to put it down when Tilby said, 'The lining there. It's split.'

Spruce pushed his fingers into the gap between the fraying silk of the lining and the soft leather and moved them about. Then he extracted a black and white passport-size photograph. Together the two men peered at it. It showed the face and neck of a man of about forty-five, his dark hair *en brosse*. The background was grey and mottled but discernibly above the man's left ear was a crucifix. Spruce stared at it intently for a moment. Then he turned and looked at Tilby.

'Makepeace,' they said together.

Spruce turned it over. There was no photographer's name on it. 'Still, given the crucifix, it couldn't be just a passport photograph.'

'We could ask his dad if he recognises it,' Tilby suggested. 'I mean it's a bit queer Tibor whatever-his-name having a photo of the murder victim in his wallet. D'you reckon it's there to tell him who he was? Help him to pick him out?'

'You mean so that he could seek him out and kill him?' Spruce's tone didn't convey disbelief, just inquiry. 'Get a copy of Tibor's statement and see what he said.'

Tilby scrolled his way through the computer screen. Spruce read over his shoulder. 'To the question did he know the murdered man, Joshua Makepeace, he said . . . he'd never met him. And to the question of where he was between six-thirty and seven he said he was looking to the soup.'

'Possibly lying in both cases,' Tilby said. 'I mean, why carry in a concealed part of your wallet the photograph of a man you don't know?'

'We've got to find Tibor,' Spruce said, his anxiety clear in his tone.

'We've sent Sergeant Yaxley down to the address Victor the manager gave us.'

'Any news?'

'Not as yet.'

'Give them a call.'

Tilby did something with his mobile. There was a lot of crackling and then, 'Derek? Super wants to know what you've got for him down Tibor's place.' There was a lot more crackling. Finally Tilby said, 'OK, hang on there a bit, I dare say the Superintendent might like to drop by and have a look himself.'

Lucy drew Theodora into the passage between the main auditorium and the entrance to the stage. She was holding her coffee in its plastic holder firmly but her hand was trembling, Theodora noticed. 'As I said, I do want to talk to you but perhaps it's best if we aren't seen together. Let's meet in the chapel next to the laundrette. See you there in five minutes.'

'Surely,' Theodora began to say, 'there's no need for such precautions?' But then she thought, A man has been killed. It wasn't random. We do not know why. Lucy is not mad, even if a shade melodramatic. Five minutes later she slipped out of the throng, turned out into the cold, dry air of the alley – Shane Lane, was it – which ended in the row of gimcrack buildings containing the chapel, the laundrette and an empty shop on the end. The laundrette was cordoned off with red and white tape but the chapel was open. Theodora waited a moment whilst Lucy finished her prayers and sat back in her seat. The place was after all consecrated.

'Good to see that the religious habits of the conference-goers have been respected,' she said to Lucy as she slipped into the chair next to her, one of four rows of three facing an altar which was a table with a white cloth and a brass cross on it. The only other decoration was a faded black and gold ikon of the Virgin and child to the south of the altar on the wall.

'Canon Oldsalmon asked them to unlock it for the Forward in Faith mass this evening. He said he was fed up with using that billiard room when there was a perfectly good chapel and Father O'Connor was quite amenable.'

Theodora, who had attended Canon Oldsalmon's mass in the billiard room at seven-thirty that morning, had rather relished the early Christian feeling of the venue. 'We must have had to use all sorts of unsuitable places when we first started,' she pointed out.

'Catacombs and such,' Lucy agreed. 'And of course when Arthur and I were in the field we attended celebrations in all sorts of queer places. I remember when we were in Umundi one time the only room large enough to accommodate us in the rainy season was a groundnut-oil processing factory. We worked round the vats of oil. However . . .'

'You said, in your note,' Theodora prompted her, 'that you heard voices in the night.'

Lucy nodded. 'Arthur thinks I'm doddering, you know.'

'Oh, I'm sure not.' Theodora hated to think of any discord between that admirable pair.

'He thinks that I miss the mission field and that I imagined I heard the Umundese language outside our window. But I didn't imagine it.'

'What exactly did you hear?' Theodora inquired.

'I heard the sound of an engine, then two men's voices. One I think was an English voice speaking in the language but his accent was good,' Lucy conceded.

'And the other?'

'The other was definitely a native speaker. A man. Not young by the timbre of it.'

'Saying what?'

'"Aparni suzeni." We are late. Hurry up.'

'And then?'

'There was some joking about the cold. Then the English speaker said, "We have to go uphill from here. It's not far. You'll soon be warm."'

'What time was all this?' Theodora asked.

'I looked at our travelling clock, it has an illuminated dial, you know, and it said a quarter past three.'

Theodora said gently, 'It's quite an innocent conversation.'

Lucy nodded. 'It would be, wouldn't it, at any time except three in the morning? And in any language except Umundese. But . . .'

'But what?'

'They weren't at ease,' Lucy said. 'They were furtive and the English speaker, I'm practically sure, was Father Martin Guard. He has such a beautiful voice, don't you think?' Lucy paused and then said, 'They're all members of the secret band, you know.'

Oh dear, Theodora thought, she really is doddering after all. Then to be quite sure she asked, 'Which band would that be?'

'Adjumentum Salvatoris.'

Theodora hesitated. That band certainly wasn't a figment of Lucy's imagination. It existed. She suspected that she herself knew members of this secretive brotherhood and, after all, it was with Adjumentum Salvatoris that Joshua

Makepeace had spent his couple of years before taking orders.

'So do you know anything about them?' Lucy asked. Was it too innocently?

Theodora said, 'Even if Martin Guard is a member of Adjumentum Salvatoris, it's not an illegal organisation. There's nothing criminal in belonging to a order of religious dedicated to good works and missionary activity.'

'Of course there isn't,' said Lucy hotly. 'We had friends who did wonderful work in all sorts of gimcrack organisations. They had a little money and they sponsored good men and women in the mission field. The Anglican communion would be infinitely poorer if they hadn't done their bits over the years. But Adjumentum Salvatoris is quite different.'

Theodora knew what she meant. 'It's secret,' she agreed.

'Our Lord was against mystery religions,' Lucy said firmly.

'The early Christians must have themselves looked very like a mystery religion to those on the outside.'

'But the rest of the Church today isn't on the outside,' Lucy objected. 'There is all the rest of us in the mainstream. And I don't agree with men taking oaths to each other.'

'The religious do.'

Theodora was aware that she was feeling around to find excuses for them. She very much didn't want the Church to be brought into bad odour or to suffer in any way because boys liked forming secret societies and dining together every now and again.

'The religious take an oath to God,' Lucy said sombrely, 'not to each other. That's quite different. And it makes for such difficulties when they are bound to each other. How can they seek truth and justice which might in some cases be distant from their brothers?'

Theodora thought she had a point. How could they

discharge their duties impartially with that sort of hidden agenda? 'What do you want me to do about it?'

'Could you check out the Umundese in this country? I don't know, ring their legation or something?'

'Why not you?'

'They'd take no notice of an old woman.' Lucy wasn't self-pitying, just matter of fact. 'And what do you know about Adjumentum Salvatoris?'

'Not much,' Theodora admitted.

'Well, I'll see what I can do about them. Then we'll share, won't we?' In the distance they could hear the sound of a door being shut. Theodora looked at her watch. 'Do you want to hear the rest of Kenneth Bloomfield?'

'Oh, I think I ought to. We may need to discuss him over lunch. And Arthur would be disappointed if I didn't.'

As soon as he saw the room Spruce knew he was too late. Tibor had left and left in a hurry. The doors of the built-in cupboard stood open and the cupboard was empty. The single bed in its rickety wooden frame was pushed out of true as though perhaps a suitcase had been pulled from beneath it. There was a mug of cold tea on the plastic-topped table beneath the window. The only decoration was a Sacred Heart oleograph over the bed. There were no personal possessions of any kind.

The house was a tall white-painted Edwardian end-of-terrace affair with a sea view at the farthest point of the long promenade. Beyond it lay the rough tenacious grass of the fields reaching towards the estuary. The house had an air of waiting to be filled. Spruce thought how very dependent the inhabitants of Highcliffe were on the season; how they seemed to simmer down and hibernate between October and April. They didn't do other things with their lives, they just waited, like boatmen for the tide, mending their nets, washing their curtains and dabbing bits of paint on to ill-prepared surfaces, until the visitors returned in the spring.

The landlady was a mere girl, thin with pale stringy hair round her shoulders, clad in a tight-fitting pink summer top and straight black skirt with a child on her arm. Tilby, Spruce could see, put her down as a tart. She couldn't make up her mind whether the invasion of the police was a nuisance or a bit of excitement in her otherwise dull life. They followed her down the stairs from the bedroom and lodged themselves in the tiny kitchen, a room cut out from the older, larger one of the ample house in order to enlarge the dining room for the lodgers.

'When did he go?'

'He come back early, tennish.'

'And when did he leave?'

'I dunno. I had to take kids down the shops.'

'How long's he lived here?'

'Three years. My mum took him just before she died. He was what I inherited, like.'

'Where'd he come from?'

'He never said. I took him for Pole. My grandad said he'd met some of them in the war when he worked on munitions in Felixstowe.'

That had seemed to be all. Spruce was angry and resentful at his own lack of speed. But what could he have done which he had not done which would have helped? He'd questioned the man as they'd questioned the scores of others at Bolly's. Apart from his foreignness he had no oddities. Nothing to indicate that he might have known Joshua Makepeace.

'When he came back here, tennish, how did he seem? I mean, was he . . . Did you think he was going to leave?'

'Skip, you mean? Well, no. I mean I wasn't watching really. He'd paid his rent for this month so I wasn't that bothered.'

'How did he pay you?' Spruce asked on a sudden intuition.

'Cash. First of the month. Very regular. I kept him because of that. It's best if they're regular. Not like some.'

'What about his habits?'

'He was very clean and orderly, like. Never made no mess. Used the bathroom very nicely. You couldn't complain.' The girl paused, then admitted, 'I used to say to him: You look as though you're a bird of passage, Mr Tibor.'

'Meaning?'

The girl considered. 'As though he wasn't staying. As though he'd never unpacked. Never got nothing to unpack. Except his picture.'

'Which picture?'

'He had one of them foreign things, woman with a bleeding heart. Horrible. But he was attached.'

Spruce digested this. 'Have you any other lodgers?'

'Guests,' she said firmly. 'We call them guests. We're a guest house not a lodging house.'

'Guests then.'

'There's only Rita, Mrs Goddard. She's been here since I was a girl. She was a friend of my Auntie Marge's. Mum let her stay on for friendship's sake.' The girl's voice was pious. 'And I hadn't the heart to get rid when Mum died. I expect she'll die here too. In the end.' She finished on a hopeful note.

'Is she in? Could we have a word?'

The girl indicated the open door and the staircase beyond.

Rita Goddard looked as though she had been well washed and then hung out to dry on a windy clothes line. She smelt of carbolic and her neat pink blouse and hand-knitted cardigan had been through the washing machine many times. But her hair was straight and wild about her head like a disorientated halo. She sat in an armchair beside the window. A black and white television in the far corner, with the sound turned low, chuntered to itself like an idiot child.

'Have you come about Tibor, Inspector?'

'Superintendent,' said Tilby. He was protective of his boss's rank. 'I'm the Inspector.'

'Big cheeses both,' said the friend of Auntie Marge.

Spruce took to her. He smiled and drew up the other chair which was of the folding canvas variety found on beaches and in gardens.

'Yes, we've come about Mr Tibor. What can you tell us about him?'

'Well, he weren't a Pole, that I can tell you,' Mrs Goddard said with conviction.

'What makes you say that?'

'My first was a Pole. Before I met Mr Goddard, that was. I was a war bride,' she added with pride. 'I met Ladislaw when we both worked in munitions in Felixstowe during the war. I wasn't above sixteen and he was very handsome. He had a moustache to die for. My dad wasn't keen but in the end we had to get married. We did in them days, you know. You couldn't take a chance and go it alone like they do nowadays. Well, anyway, I'd picked up a word or two of Polish. You can't help but pick up a bit, can you?' She sounded as though the language was a disease she'd valiantly resisted. 'Anyway, I tried them on Tibor.'

'And?'

'Not a flicker,' Mrs Goddard said triumphantly.

'Do you know what he was?'

Mrs Goddard ruminated. This took the form of running both her hands through her hair which made it stand up from her head all the more. 'I saw his passport and stuff, visa would it be, one time.'

'Where?'

'It was in his room. I'd gone across to ask him if he wanted to watch the telly. There was something I thought he might like. Football, I shouldn't wonder. It always is nowadays.'

'And?'

'I knocked but there was no reply so I put my head round the door. It was lying there on the floor and I just happened to glance. He's Turkish.'

'There's no passport in his room now,' Spruce probed.

'You go and look at the floor round by the bedhead on the left-hand side and maybe you'll get lucky.'

Tilby lifted the bed. The sergeant rolled back the carpet and Spruce carefully raised the floorboard. He fumbled for a moment and then came up clutching a plastic bag. He shook the contents out on the dingy green counterpane and they looked at the loot. There, sure enough, was a passport with the Turkish cipher on it and another with the British arms, together with a visa and another card in Turkish which no one could read. Spruce looked critically at the British passport for a moment and then his expression changed. 'Well, I'm beggared . . .'

'What's up?'

'George the Forger. Look.' Spruce brought a magnifying glass from his breast pocket and handed it to Inspector Tilby.

The man shook his head. 'It's no good, sir. I haven't your eye and it wasn't my case when you got him.'

'I'm certain it's his work. I must have studied scores of his artworks before we got him in the end. Anyway, send this lot to the arts and crafts people and see what they say. But I'll be disappointed in them if they don't confirm. Then you can get on to—'

'Immigration. Yes, I'll see to that.' Tilby was excited. It looked as though things were beginning to move after twenty-four hours of sitting about in Bolly's nibbling their fingernails. He could easily imagine a racket in forged passports ending in murder, much more easily than anything to do with the man being a priest.

'Would George be out yet or is this one of his "taken into consideration" offences, would you say?'

'The sergeant will be checking George's present abode,' Tilby assured him. Then he thought he might as well chance his arm. After all this was a genuine step forward. 'How would having a forged passport and so on connect up with his also having a photograph of Reverend Makepeace?'

'Maybe the Revd was giving him pastoral care?' Spruce said.

'Looking after him, like?'

'Got it in one, Inspector.'

'So where now?'

'I think we'd better go back to base and have a film show.'

Theodora had not returned for the second part of Kenneth Bloomfield's address. She saw Lucy safely back to her seat, made as though to take up her own and then slipped round to the exit. She wondered what Spruce was doing and where? She thought of the old man, Captain Makepeace, his initial eagerness that his son's murderer should be found and then his cooling from that ardour as the interview had gone on.

Lucy's conversation, too, worried her. She had said that Martin Guard's words, if they were Martin's, were perfectly innocent and so they were but what was he doing at that time of the night or day? And was Lucy right that he was speaking Umundese? Then there was all that about Adjumentum Salvatoris. That at least she thought she might be able to do some research on. The person who would know all about that was back in her own parish. The Reverend Canon Gilbert Racy of St Sylvester's Foundation, next door to her own church in Betterhouse, sat as a spider at the centre of a web of gossip and friendships which put him in touch with all the activities of the Church especially as it concerned the Catholic wing and particularly the more bizarre or eccentric bits of that wing. Theodora thought of him as a character out of Firbank, which was unfair, she acknowledged, because he was a faithful priest, disciplined in his life and exemplary in his attention to his duties.

She looked round for somewhere from which she could make a long phone call without being interrupted.

CHAPTER SEVEN

Pictures from the Past

There was no need to draw the curtains in Harries Bar. The November light was already beginning to fade when Spruce placed a chair for Theodora and Tilby fiddled knowledgably with the projector. The plastic bag had yielded a film-tape and a video cassette. Theodora smoothed the plastic bag on the table; at the bottom she felt a slight thickening.

Tilby said, 'Here it comes.' The machine began to whirr. 'An amateur job,' he added.

The film was black and white of poor quality, grainy and indistinct. There was a shivering line of white flashes and then the title in gothic character, 'The Art of the Jester'. The tape ground on, clicking and shuddering, the focus swinging round a number of objects arranged on a table covered by the heavy folds of an old-fashioned velvet tablecloth. The camera picked out a cap and bells, a feather duster, a censer, a candle, a dunce's cap, what looked like a pestle and mortar but which Theodora recognised as a bowl for shaving soap and a shaving brush. 'Tools of the Trade', announced the gothic script. Finally the camera tracked into the middle of the table and focused on a crucifix. Spruce leaned forward. 'It's the one,' he said.

'Which one?' Theodora asked.

Spruce took the photograph from Tibor's wallet and pushed it across to Theodora. 'Freeze it a minute,' he said to Tilby. Tilby arrested the progress of the tape. Together they studied the photograph with its crucifix. The wood of the cross was dark, either stained or perhaps ebony; the pale figure nailed to it perhaps ceramic or ivory. Spruce looked back at the screen. 'Can you enlarge it?'

Tilby did something technical and the crucifix filled the screen, the same dark wood and with the light figure on it.

'It's the same,' said Theodora with conviction and unusual emotion.

'Roll it on.' Spruce nodded to Tilby. The three of them strained forward towards the screen. The background got lighter and the words flashed across the screen. 'Ploys and Positions'. There followed a series of frames showing Joshua in Pierrot costume. He began slowly almost parodying the slow motion of action replays. His physical control was phenomenal. Gradually the speed increased and the movements turned to tumbling, juggling, spinning and leaping. The movements were fast and assured. Theodora was reminded of Marceau, whom she had seen in her youth. The pace and quality of the movement was astonishing, precise yet frenetic, his dramatic projection and the range and vocabulary of physical movement well beyond the scope of the amateur.

Suddenly the full pity of his death hit her. Here was quality, talent not frequent in human society, untimely wiped out. She could feel the two policemen forming a relationship with the flashing figure on the screen and beginning to be drawn into his aura. The last frame was a close-up of the face of the clown, the make-up dead white, the head bare but the short hair standing up as it had been in the photograph with again the crucifix visible above and behind him. 'The End', read the frame. There was silence.

'He's eloquent,' said Spruce after a moment.

'He's good,' Tilby agreed.

'Where would he learn techniques like that?' Spruce raised the obvious question. The two policemen turned to Theodora.

'The Eastern European tradition,' Theodora began hesitantly. 'That is, the countries of the former Soviet empire ran state circuses. They had schools attached.'

'That couple of years he was supposed to be with Adjumentum Salvatoris,' Spruce began. There was silence.

'And then of course Tibor,' said Tilby.

'Who wasn't a Pole,' Spruce quoted.

'He came into the country how and from where?'

'He had a double passport,' Spruce filled Theodora in. 'Turkish and British. Only the British one might be a fake.' Theodora nodded. She thought of her telephone calls to Canon Racy and the Umundese legation. Should she share these with Spruce or should she wait and see how things panned out?

'One or two of the former Soviet states border on Turkey,' Theodora pointed out. 'Someone's going to have to track through Immigration.'

'They're already doing Tibor,' Tilby said.

'They'll need to check Joshua Makepeace out as well. Where did he spend the last two years before he became a priest?'

'How about contacting Adjumentum Salvatoris?'

The two policemen both looked at Theodora.

'Well,' she said, 'I have done a little research. I rang a colleague of mine who's up in religious orders, Gilbert Racy. He lives near us in Betterhouse at the Foundation of St Sylvester. However, for some reason he wasn't as forthcoming as he usually is. He told me not much more than we might guess from what we've learned already. It's an all-male order founded in the 1930s by a South African

Anglican priest called Bornglass who died in 1960. It's open to priests only. It has houses all over the world. Its work is mostly in refugee camps. The only interesting thing I picked up from Gilbert Racy is that it attracts a certain amount of envy because it appears to be well funded. It's also secretive in its workings.'

'Masonic,' Tilby said. 'We've got a few of them in the force.'

'How about looking at the video?' Theodora nudged them on. 'And I think there was something else in the bag as well.' Tilby looked embarrassed and fumbled in the depths. He drew out a brown A4-size envelope. It had a Dutch stamp on it postmarked Hevenningen. And the date was the 16 November, the address read Lt. J. Makepeace, The Boatyard, Braden Loke, Medwich.

'Which would mean it probably got to old man Makepeace's place about last Friday,' Tilby conjectured.

'Just in time to be picked up by Joshua when he came on Sunday evening, as his father said,' Spruce concluded.

'And inside?' Theodora reminded them.

Spruce shook it out on to the table. There was a single folded piece of paper, what looked like a sketch map. Spruce smoothed it out on the table and the three heads pored over it. It was Spruce who recognised it first. It was a map of the estuary showing the river winding all the way up to Medwich fifteen miles inland. At the mouth of the estuary, standing a little out to sea, the light ship was clearly marked and so, inland, was Makepeace's boatyard. Written down the right-hand side of the page were a list of numbers which they all recognised as Ordnance Survey map references and against them were written times. At the bottom of the page was the date 27 November.

'Day after tomorrow,' said Tilby.

'How much sailing did Joshua do?' Spruce asked no one in particular.

'You reckon it's a map for a pleasure jaunt?'

'Could be. On the other hand . . .' Spruce came to a conclusion. 'Take a copy, get the fingerprints checked and phone it through to Marriot at Felixstowe Customs. Say I'd like to have a word this evening about seven, if he's free.'

'Did you notice,' Theodora said, 'the writing of the numbers? Map references are in one handwriting and the times written beside them are in another hand? One has the continental sevens with the bar across the middle, the other is in the English style without it.'

'Makepeace sent the map to friends with references and they sent it back with times?' Spruce suggested.

'You think someone's bringing something in?' Theodora inquired.

'I think we need to know just how much sailing Makepeace did and at what times.'

'Would his father know?'

'Depends how much he was in his son's confidence, and what Joshua used for a boat if he did sail. He could have used another yard or he could keep his boat, if any, somewhere else.'

'Did you see anything seaworthy at Makepeace's yard?' Tilby asked. Theodora realised that he would have liked to have been on that trip with his boss and felt guilty that it was she who had accompanied Spruce.

'It was too dark to see exactly what he had there,' Spruce assured him. 'Go back yourself tomorrow morning, have a good look round and see if there's anything Joshua could have put to sea in. Have a word with his father.'

'This business of Joshua not living anywhere,' Theodora said, 'and yet his sending his father cards from ports "which he might know", would that suggest that he might actually have a boat as a base? I really find it difficult to believe that someone doesn't have any place to call their own. For example that collection of artefacts we've just seen and his costumes.'

'Does he have a bank account anywhere?' Spruce asked Tilby.

'We haven't traced one.'

'Surely you can't run a business nowadays without storing money somewhere?'

'On the other hand if you don't want to have your affairs known then doing without a bank account is a good idea,' Spruce pointed out.

Theodora glanced for a last time at the map and made every attempt to memorise it. 'What about the video?' she invited them.

The video was a much more professional affair than the film. It was in colour and the person taking it had had some experience. It showed a wedding and then a baptism. There was a soundtrack which caught the murmurs of the congregation without actually picking up individual conversations and in parts some background music had been added. The first episode, the wedding, was a morning-coat affair. It was set in a large flint and glass fenland church. It might have been shot more from the point of view of the happy couple than to show off Joshua's art. He figured darting in and out of the wedding guests. After a bit he was glimpsed shadowing the best man. He walked with solemn importance behind him carrying his feather duster. Then just before the ring was due to be given, he deftly lifted the ring from the pocket of the best man and flicked it high into the air. The soundtrack died. There was a breathless moment of silence and all waited to hear the ring strike the stone floor of the church. The camera tracked its flight high into the air almost touching the roof thirty feet above them before it began to fall. Then with one agile movement Joshua deftly scooped it before it hit the floor, bowed to the couple and restored it to the best man.

'Make what you like of that as a piece of symbolism.' Theodora was appreciative.

'Seems to say it all,' Spruce agreed.

'Must be very strong in the wrist to throw a light thing like a wedding ring so high.' Tilby had his own standards of excellence.

The christening was a rather different affair. It appeared to take place in a modern chapel. The parents and congregation were informally dressed. The baby was carried by its mother. At first Joshua couldn't be seen. Then the camera tracked in amongst the guests and caught him peering over the edge of the font, his eyes at the level of its top. He might have been indicating a baby's eye view of the proceedings. Just before the moment of the pouring of water came, Joshua gently levered the child from his mother's arms, stooped and kissed him. Then he handed him to the girl next to him. The camera caught the girl hesitating and then, catching the mood and the meaning, she too gently took up the child, kissed him and so handed him on to the man next to her. The child went round the five people grouped round the font, presumably the godparents, until he arrived back at the mother who handed him to the priest. 'He had much to teach us about liturgy.' Theodora was sombre; in truth, she felt near tears. She felt an unaccustomed twinge of anger. If she could help to bring to justice the killers of Joshua Makepeace she would do so.

Tilby brought the showing to an end. He stayed it on the last frame of the happy parents and their friends coming out of the chapel door. In the background could be seen a group of what looked like tank stops but which Theodora recognised without difficulty as the science faculty of Felixstowe University.

'Look,' she said suddenly. Spruce and Tilby looked.

'What's up?'

'Wasn't he in the other film, the one of the wedding?'

'Who?' Tilby asked.

'Third from the left. Kenneth Bloomfield. Rather American dressing, shiny blue suit and collarless cream silk shirt.'

'Go back to the wedding,' Spruce told Tilby. 'Where did you see him?' he asked Theodora.

'When he spins the ring, don't watch the ring, look to the left of the best man.'

There he was again, his eyes fixed on Joshua. Kenneth was dressed more conventionally this time in dapper grey tailcoat and grey stock.

'Gets about a bit,' Tilby suggested.

'We need to know the provenance of both those videos.'

Theodora made the obvious comment. 'Since Kenneth was in both of them, perhaps he might know.'

Spruce looked consideringly for a moment. Then he glanced at his watch. It was half past six. 'Where would Kenneth be, would you say?'

'I heard him say he was going back to the university after lunch. I gather he didn't want to involve himself more deeply in our conference.'

Tilby looked hopeful. 'You stay here, Jon,' Spruce said, 'and get the fingerprints and the Customs people organised. Theodora and I will just take a trip to academia.'

'You can't come in,' said the university equivalent of Jason. The entrance, however, and porter's lodge were more impressive than that to Bolly's, the porter's uniform more traditional. He had a peaked hat and a braided jacket. Below the level of the counter could be seen a pair of plaid trousers. Spruce showed his warrant card.

'Ye must know, Inspector, that we sort out our own student problems here. And ye ken we don't have that many here. They're a law-abiding and God-fearing lot of young lads and lassies.'

This was so unexpected and indeed unlikely that Theodora supposed he must be drunk.

'We're looking for Dr Kenneth Bloomfield,' said Spruce.

'Och, if it's the teachers you're looking for, I couldna give you my word on them.'

What is it about being a porter which makes them all quite impossible, Theodora wondered. She remembered her own time at university where they had all, without exception, been disobliging. Some of the older ones, indeed, had not caught up with the fact that their colleges were open to, indeed inhabited by, women. Something to do with power, she supposed.

'Where might we find him?' Spruce, who presumably had to deal with far more of this sort of thing than she did, seemed unfazed.

'Yonder,' said the Scottish character actor, gesturing as though to a distant glen. 'First right, second left, then follow ye nose.'

Spruce seemed content with this.

Theodora said, 'Last time I came here the dons' flats were behind the chapel which, it seems' – she peered through the windscreen – 'is marked.'

Spruce edged the car forward down the unlit road and followed the signs. The university had been built in the sixties by an architect who intended it to make his name. His method of doing this was to design in concrete a set of modules which had wide bases and diminishing subsequent floors culminating in a single glass house on the top. The impression, as was frequently remarked, was that of a ziggurat. At night, as now, the blocks were probably at their prettiest. The lights from the different receding floors made them look festive, like lanterns. In between the blocks placed at irregular angles to each other, banks of scrub and small ornamental trees, leafless now and looking as though they had been knitted out of barbed wire, gave their journey a sense of danger and assault. Finally, Spruce brought the Rover to a halt outside a more conventional two-storey block with an illuminated sign so close to the ground that the uncut grass almost obscured it saying, 'Private. Staff only. No students.'

'There's a lot of "keep out" round here,' Spruce remarked.

'And in life in general,' Theodora agreed.

They weren't through yet either. The security arrangements were formidable. There was a steel grille gate, mercifully folded back, then an entryphone and a list of names.

'Yes,' said a voice, which Theodora recognised as Kenneth Bloomfield's, answering their ring.

'Superintendent Spruce, Medwich CID, and the Reverend Theodora Braithwaite.'

Theodora thought what an ill-assorted couple they sounded. The door beeped at them and then hissed open. There was no indoor light in the hall and they stumbled up the shiny metal staircase and along an uncarpeted wood floor which smelled strongly of silicone polish. Kenneth Bloomfield was in shirt-sleeves, the collarless collar area open to display a good growth of black hair. The room had windows at both ends, a computer at a table in the middle and books on all available walls and surfaces.

'The internet's all very well for our sociological brothers,' he said by way of conversation, 'but if you want to progress beyond information to theory, principle, and, dare I say it, virtue and wisdom, the small screen is not a great help.'

His tone, Theodora thought, was constrained and nervous. She'd last seen him holding an audience of clergy with no trace of nerves. Now his diction wavered between American and caricature don. Still, she concurred with his sentiment and felt it was a good opening. Whisky was produced which further aided conversation. Finally Spruce embarked. 'Joshua Makepeace,' he began.

'Was a remarkable man,' Kenneth said.

'Have you known him long?'

'He was chaplain here when I came. He left after a year to pursue his ministry as a jester.'

'How well did you know him?'

'We shared certain interests.'

'Such as?' Spruce could see it was going to be a long night.

Kenneth Bloomfield reflected. 'My family, my granddad's generation, were Jewish. That means we were outsiders. And of course that leaves a mark on the way we think, on our fears. Even when we converted, I guess it's hard to throw off a history of a couple of thousand years of persecution. We compensate, you know. We try very hard in those spheres that are open to us, in which we feel safe.' He gestured to the book-lined cell. Theodora suddenly saw the books as a sort of padding, a defence against a world which might at any moment turn hostile.

'And the connection with Joshua?'

'He seemed to know about being outside things. When he was chaplain he looked out for those on the outside, what in the States they call losers, the no-hopers. He'd go round and get them going. The weak, the marginalised, the bullied. That's not too common in professional Christian circles.'

Theodora noticed that he havered between the American diction and intonation which he clearly liked and the more formal and abstract English one which older members of university staffs still speak. Couldn't he make up his mind who he was? How marginalised was he himself?

Spruce digested this. 'You appear on a couple of video films, one of a wedding and one of a baptism. Could you just fill us in on the provenance?'

'I go to a lot of weddings, Superintendent. I'm of an age

when my students are entering that state. They like to have me there sometimes. I guess I add a bit of weight to the proceedings. Not as many baptisms. Yet.'

'The baptism seems to have been taking place in the university chapel,' Theodora said.

Kenneth thought for a moment. 'Last summer. The Gronewskis had their young man done.'

'The Gronewskis being who exactly?'

'She's English, he's from what used to be Yugoslavia.'

'A British citizen?' Spruce asked formally.

'He was here when the country split and he satisfied the Immigration people that if he went back he'd be killed.'

'Was he a student?'

'Yep, he was one of ours. Reading engineering, in his second year.'

'And where would he be now?'

'He's doing his placement year.'

'Placement?'

'Engineering students do a year with a firm as part of the practical side of the course.'

'Where's he gone?'

'Edgecombe and Makepeace. They're marine and agricultural engineers in Felixstowe and they've got a head office in Medwich.'

'So they have,' said Spruce the local man, 'now you mention it. What's the Makepeace interest?'

'Old man Makepeace was partner in the firm before he retired.'

'And do the Gronewskis live on the campus?'

'Oh, yes. They need the sort of support that a communal life can provide. Crèche and so on.'

'So when he was chaplain Joshua gathered people round him, people who weren't too successful.'

Kenneth nodded. 'It wasn't simply a matter of looking after the isolates. He was gregarious. He was a good chaplain. Because he wasn't married he could give all his time to the job. I'd reckon a lot of people of all kinds had reason to be grateful to Josh.'

'Would you say that there were any relationships formed during that time which might lead to his being killed ten years later?'

Kenneth leaned forward in his chair. 'Look,' he said, 'Josh wasn't a homosexual, he didn't take drugs, there were no criminals on campus as far as I know. If he was killed, murdered, it's just as likely to be either the result of relationships formed much more recently or else it was random.'

'How do you mean "random"?'

Kenneth seemed to run out of steam. 'Oh, I don't know. He got around a lot, given what he did. Could he have bumped into something by accident, become a risk to someone, had to be silenced type thing?'

Theodora thought this was quite acute of Kenneth. Was he guessing or did he know something?

'And what about the other thing, the wedding?' Spruce took up the final thread. 'Where did it take place?'

'It looked like a fen church,' Theodora felt it was her province. 'Anglo-Catholic rite by the look of it. And summer by the frocks.'

Spruce smiled companionably at her. He felt it had been a good idea to bring her. He valued specialist knowledge. It cut down time in the long run.

Kenneth seemed to be happier to chat about his social relations. He thought a bit. 'It sounds like last summer too. Rupert Young got married to Tamasin. He's the Vice-chancellor's youngest. There was a big do out at Wrattingthorpe. Lot of money spent.'

'Joshua was known to the family?'

'He was an old sailing buddy of Rupert's. They used to race a bit and make the odd Channel crossing together.

Joshua was a better, in the sense of safer, sailor than Rupert, obviously the Navy background and so on.'

'And Martin Guard?' Theodora said. 'Was he a friend of Rupert's?'

'Guard?' Kenneth looked startled for a moment. 'Oh yes, yes of course they knew each other.'

'I asked,' Theodora said, 'because I thought I recognised him as the priest conducting the wedding.'

'Oh, could be,' Kenneth was noncommittal.

'And finally,' Theodora said gently, 'I wondered if you knew who took the videos of the wedding or the christening, by any chance?'

'That was my brother, David. He does these things for a bit of fun from time to time. It keeps us in touch, you might say.'

'You don't see a lot of your brother normally?'

'Families, brothers, do drift apart, I find.'

CHAPTER EIGHT

Fens

A note addressed to Theodora Braithwaite had been pinned to the messages board on Wednesday night. It said:

> Dear Theo, I hear you're conferencing at Bolly's. Heaven help you. Have you a moment to spare? I wondered if you'd care to come and have a bite perhaps tomorrow evening. One or two family things I'd value your opinion on. Say about seven? Don't worry if you can't manage but perhaps give me another time convenient to yourself. I'm not on the phone. I find it such a confounded nuisance and interruption to my work. But if you want to get a message through, Mrs Blain, Father Sentinel's housekeeper at the Old Rectory down the road, doesn't mind acting as post box. Anyway, looking forward to seeing you,
> Yr afftnte cousin,
> Randolph Trimming

Theodora considered this ambiguous message. It was so very different in tone from the first letter she'd had from him. There he'd shown all the signs of a hunted fox declining the invitation of hounds to have a bit of a run out. Here he was positively pursuing her. Then, there was the mysterious bit about advice on family matters. The whole point about Randolph Trimming's family affairs was that he showed no signs at all of paying the least attention to the advice of his family on any important matter. He'd married in haste (and repented at leisure) a South American with neither family nor money. He'd neglected his son to the point that the lad had had an inadequate education and now had a criminal conviction. He himself had neither a career nor the use of honourable leisure for public service. It was all very unBraithwaite-like, as Canon Hugh had on more than one occasion pointed out to him.

So now what? Amid her other interests Theodora was half inclined to write back and say she'd be delighted to visit after the conference ended. That had, after all, been her original plan. Two things stopped her. One was the thought of the housekeeper having to leg it up the hill from the Old Rectory, the other was the brief glimpse she'd had on Tuesday night of her cousin caught in the headlights of the van at The Buccaneer. Did his father's letter have to do with his son's friends? If so, she must go, of course. The notion of duty to family was strong. What would her father have wished her to do? What would Canon Hugh have advised? There was no room for doubt. She'd go to supper.

She had detached the letter from the board in Warm Welcome at seven a.m. before most conference-goers were about. It must have come in last night and, of course, not expecting any messages and having her mind on other things, she'd not checked. So she mentally rearranged her plans for the day.

By the end of Wednesday Theodora had become aware that there were several different rhythms operating in the conference. They resembled competing currents in an estuary where, it is said, the tide could be going out in the middle of the tideway while it is still coming in under the banks and in the drainage dykes. At seven-thirty a.m. the Catholic element, small in number but shoulder to shoulder in compactness, the priests uniformly dressed in black suits with thin white clerical collars, held a mass in the tiny RC chapel. Canon Oldsalmon celebrated, Father Sentinel and Father Martin Guard concelebrated. No woman entered the sanctuary. At eight the Affirming Catholics led by the Archdeacon held a Prayer Book Eucharist in The Kowlabouse with candles and a good choir, not as many as the Evangelicals but not as few as the Catholics. A woman served from the sanctuary. At eight-fifteen the Evangelicals, much larger in number, gathered in The OK Corale with a couple of Chris Teane's young men on guitars for an ASB Morning Prayer plus supplement where they waited on the Spirit. It was not too easy to see who were priests and who not and, indeed, who were women and who not. In the course of the morning's seminars and group work Evangelicals would tender their agreement with the speakers by ejaculating 'Amen, hallelujah'. The Catholics and Affirming Catholics did not join in. At twelve the Catholics stopped whatever they were doing to recite the Angelus. Some of the Affirming Catholics joined in if it wasn't too disruptive. All parties joined together for lunch. At six p.m. both sorts of Catholics went to the bar. The Evangelicals held a rousing prayer meeting with a steel band and choruses.

Theodora, trying to be impartial, went to as many of these acts of worship as possible. There were things to praise in each, she felt. Just occasionally, however, she found the choruses of the Evangelicals with their endless simple verbal repetitions tedious. She was embarrassed, too, by their tendency to speak of Jesus as though he was a pop star. At ten-thirty, after the business of the day was concluded and before retiring, she attended Compline, a non-liturgical celebration whose dignity, resignation and quietness drew men and women from all traditions to its tranquil cadences.

She was not sure whether this diversity was a sign of weariness or stamina in Anglican life. Her feeling was that the differences were more emphasised than they need be, that it was a pity there was no single celebration which united people, that there was no encouragement to them to sort out a common ground or help them to understand why others differed from them.

She mentioned this to Archdeacon Treadwell as they came out of the first morning session on Thursday on 'Mission and Outreach for Young Britain for the Millennium'.

'It makes our task well-nigh impossible,' the Archdeacon agreed. He'd spent an hour and a half being told in effect that he was too old to be any use in the Church. Chris Teane had not spared him and he'd assembled a team who, to the Archdeacon, looked like thugs with no hair, heavy leathers and studs in their ears and noses. He felt guilty and resentful. It was hardly his fault that he was sixty-two and that the Church had promoted him simply because his grandfather had been a Bishop and he was known to be a competent committee man. 'Bishops are supposed to be focuses of unity but that doesn't seem to work any more. It's left to us and I have to admit there are times when it's difficult to know which way to turn. I see things called acts of worship which look simply like new age meetings.'

'The one arranged for our final act on Saturday on the beach called, I think, "Sea Breezes", looks as though it might be liturgically innovative.' Theodora offered him a chance to let off steam.

The Archdeacon snorted. He knew she was a safe woman. He'd known her father. 'Peach, Teane and Worsted are organising it. And they've asked that blithering idiot Daniel Ripe to help as well. They indicated early on that they wouldn't be expecting my help. So it'll be a caring-and-sharing-of-sticky-emotion do, waiting on the Spirit to see if He'd like a prayer. I've come to hate the phrases "I was led", "I didn't feel comfortable". A kind of Full Monty of the spiritual life. On the other hand all this Forward in Faith stuff, walking out when the Bishop is celebrating because he ordains women – it's so bad mannered. Christ ate with sinners. You'd think they might manage to do the same. They don't have to take the sacrament from a woman's hands if they don't think it's consecrated. They can sit in their stalls and think of other things if it pleases them.'

The Archdeacon stopped, aware that he had been un-archdeaconly. He had said what he felt for once. Teane was right, he was getting too old for the Church as currently constituted. Time he retired. The two of them were passing close to the perimeter fence of the holiday camp. The fresh keen wind was whipping in off the sea and there were gulls riding the gusts with the abandonment of things properly designed for their environment.

Theodora realised that the strain of the conference was getting to the Archdeacon. 'And then,' he went on, 'this terrible business of the murder of Makepeace. The police don't seem to be making any progress and there are too many local press men round the place who are interested in murder but aren't interested in religion.'

Theodora felt guilty about this. It wasn't rational, of course, but she had come to feel personally responsible in some way for the police inquiry. She knew that matters had in fact moved on. After they had returned from Kenneth Bloomfield's the previous night, Tilby and she had pooled information which had come in in the course of the evening. Slowly a picture had begun to come together.

There had been reports from Marriot the Customs man at Felixstowe docks. There had been further work on who had been in the area of the laundrette between six-thirty p.m. and seven on Monday evening. The two Italian girls had sworn that Tibor had been out of the kitchen at that time. Jason had been questioned again and had agreed that there had been a momentary amnesia on his part and that he had actually been late on duty and so had taken a short cut, as he put it, under the wire, to get to his entrance box and this had led him via the area of the laundrette. They had questioned Martin Guard again on the strength of Oldsalmon thinking he had seen him in that area at that time but Guard had not cracked. Indeed he'd done a good forensic job on suggesting that Canon Oldsalmon's eyesight was not what it once was. Though of course a first-rate priest. At the time in question he had not yet arrived at the camp and had been negotiating the difficult rush-hour traffic and the horrendous one-way system of Highcliffe which in the end landed him up on the wrong side of the camp at about seven. Jason on the gate said he saw him but now thinks he may have been mistaken.

About midnight Spruce had summarised, 'So the picture so far is that we have three people who could have killed Joshua in the right place at the right time but none of them so far as we know has a motive. On the other hand, from the point of view of Joshua's own private life and career' – he waved his arm towards Inspector Tilby like a conductor bringing in the second violins – 'what do we have from Marriot?'

'Marriot's very knowledgeable,' Tilby said. 'He knows all the river traffic and the private vessels. Makepeace senior has a boat, a thirty-foot ketch with an engine, suitable for estuary work, *The Admiral Hardy*, which he keeps at his yard. His son used to sail it when he was based at the university. Less often of late.'

'And Makepeace junior?'

'Had a Firefly for racing. In addition they had a small

cabin cruiser called *The Pike*, which Marriot hasn't seen for some time.'

'Like how long?'

'Like six months. He thinks they may have sold it on but doesn't know where or who to.'

'And what about the trade?' Spruce ticked his list and moved on.

'They're certain there is something coming in on a regular basis.'

'Not going through Customs?'

'Nope.'

'What sort of stuff?'

'Illegal substances.'

Theodora wondered if the police ever said 'drugs'; there was something genteel and also sinister about the periphrasis.

'Source?'

'Cypriot seaman found dead in the dock at the beginning of the year with specially made packets in the toe-cap of his sea boots.'

'Why not for his personal use?'

'Could be but it was unrefined. Would have to go through a chemist's before it could be used or sold.'

'Do they know where it's coming from?'

'The man's ship was from Holland.'

Theodora took this one in. She found herself saying, 'I can't believe that Joshua Makepeace was involved in drug-running from Holland.'

She saw she'd made a false step. In Tilby's eyes there was no such thing as an innocent man or a class of people above suspicion. She looked at Spruce whose expression gave nothing away.

'He need not have been involved. He might merely have stumbled on it somehow.' She stopped. She realised how very much what she had seen on video of Joshua's art had made him into a hero. She did not want him to have been involved in any wrongdoing.

'What did you learn about Makepeace from Bloomfield?' Tilby offered it as a tactful alternative.

Spruce looked at Theodora. 'What did we learn?' His tone was kind. He wanted to reassure her.

'That he was a good chaplain with a ministry to those young people who found it difficult to fit into university life.' She realised as she said it that she was putting her finger on a constituency for drug users.

'And that he was himself a bit of a loner. No special friends, lived on campus, apparently a celibate.' Spruce topped off the picture both of a stereotypical murderer and a stereotypical victim. Theodora felt a wave of tiredness come over her. Spruce glanced at the two of them. 'Still to come in, the forensic on Tibor's knife and coat.'

'If it was Makepeace's blood on the coat we'd have a case,' Tilby said reasonably.

'We'd have circumstantial evidence but no motive.' Spruce was more cautious. 'Anyone could plant both knife and coat if they wanted to incriminate Tibor. So what are we doing about picking Tibor up?'

'There's a call out on the national network. He hasn't got either of his passports so he'll be a bit pushed to get out by the normal routes.'

'We don't know how many passports he's got,' Spruce pointed out. 'And that reminds me. Who's seeing George the Forger?'

'I've got a date with him in Wakefield tomorrow,' Tilby said.

'Wakefield. What on earth did they want to put him up there for?'

'Nice comfortable place for a gentleman like George. He's got relations in the area, I understand.'

'Trust George,' said Spruce respectfully.

And that had been that. Spruce and Tilby had turned off the lights and left a duty sergeant in the lounge bar eating some of Victor's excellent sandwiches and making lists from the police computer records of chemists with criminal records capable of refining heroin for medical use. Theodora had returned to her chalet and planned her next day's activity.

After her unbuttoned conversation with the Archdeacon, therefore, she'd gone for coffee with a purpose. The problem of transport had exercised her. How was she to follow up her plans without it? She thought of Victor. A fixer if ever she recognised one. He was, as she expected, on duty overseeing the coffee distribution.

'How are you managing without a chef?'

Victor saw he needed to reassure a guest. 'Absolutely no problem.' He sounded cheerful. 'I've got an NVQ in Catering,' he explained modestly. 'I'm doing lunch and the evening today. Tomorrow HQ is sending a replacement from stock. They usually keep one or two up their sleeves for emergencies like this.'

Theodora wondered how often they had murders at Bolly's.

'Sounds as though we shall be well looked after. You don't happen to know anywhere I could borrow or hire a bicycle, do you? I thought I might try and get a bit of exercise this afternoon.'

This was right up Victor's street. 'Borrow mine,' he said promptly. 'I shan't be needing it till this evening owing to my efforts for dinner. It's a bit on the old side but it's stable and trustworthy.'

So here she was on a bright November afternoon doing what she most enjoyed, getting about the country. She'd left the town by the Felixstowe road, the same she'd taken with Spruce on Tuesday evening on their expedition to Captain Makepeace's yard. Instead of turning right towards the boatyard she turned left and headed inland down B roads and later no roads at all but unmade tracks perched high above the drains. She remembered her childhood holidays and how when she got lost and asked the way, the answer had always ended with the advice from a native to 'go cross the drain'. Now, however, she was properly equipped. Every now and again she drew up and checked the map she'd drawn from memory from the one in the brown envelope from Holland in the carrier bag containing the Jester video. She matched it against a detailed Ordnance Survey map which showed every farmstead and dyke. And weaving its way through the heart was the River Med, still open to modest traffic, now glimpsed, now disappearing between the occasional clump of windbent trees as it meandered from the estuary to Medwich fifteen miles inland.

The beauty of the fens caught her. The land stretched flat to the horizon in every direction. On each skyline was the tower of a fenland church. In between ran huge fields of black earth or, where there was no earth, brown and silvery-grey reeds caught now by the wintry sun. For a moment she thought of leaving Betterhouse and London and taking a nice quiet country living. But of course there was no such thing as a nice quiet country living, they all had their problems, their hatreds and antagonisms which in country areas, she knew, were carried on rancorously from generation to generation. She remembered being told how the people of the village of Markbeech would not speak to the people in the village of Hallthorpe six miles up the road because they had been on different sides in the Civil War. People weren't different just because they lived in beautiful surroundings. And in any case not everyone saw the fens as beautiful. But to Theodora their purity and symmetry of line, their austerity of colour were her ideal. There was no traffic to speak of. She'd passed a tractor with a load of sugar beet and had been overtaken by one car travelling at speed, its heavy Germanic suspension making light work of the thin tarmac of the road.

It was nearly three o'clock. It had taken her longer than she'd supposed to get this far. Though the day had been bright, by now the sun was a red disc in the west and there were clouds coming up from the east. She reckoned she had about an hour of not very good daylight before her mission would become impossible. She consulted the sketch map once more and set off at a cracking pace.

The bicycle, a man's solid old-fashioned sports variety predating the mountain bike craze, shuddered and pitched as she left even the semblance of a cart track, lifted it over a style and headed down beside a stunted hedge towards a copse of trees. At the end of the field the path became soggy with rank pools and hemp grass, its purple flowers now brown and withered. The trees, willow and poplar, crowded out the light overhead and then parted. One last push through the adherent ooze, and there it was, much as she remembered it.

The stretch of water was khaki-coloured, silvery and still as a pitted glass mirror in an ancient hall. It was hemmed in on three sides by tall calumus bull rushes. Theodora looked carefully about her. At first she could see nothing of interest, nothing that did not pertain to the natural world. The air was colder than when she had set out. There was no birdsong, though at a distance she thought she caught the low throb of an engine, perhaps a barge making its way upstream on the main river to Medwich. Carefully she made her way round the edge of the broad, heaving the bike over the marshy bits.

Then she saw it, low in the water riding from a mud weight let down from the stern about ten yards out from the reed bed, a twenty-foot cabin cruiser, the cabin small, the open hold long indicating a working boat probably able to deal with an estuary. It was clinker built and painted grey. A couple of tyres acting as fenders were suspended halfway down the hull at the cabin end. It looked quiet and efficient like a fenland fish. Painted on the stern in black lettering in the fading light Theodora could just see the name: *The Pike*.

The question was, how to get out to it. She pushed on round the water until she stood side on to the port bow. The reeds here had been beaten down, as it seemed to Theodora, fairly recently. There was a short hard extending a yard or two into the water and at the end of it, moored by a rope which was attached to the boat, floated a half-submerged raft. Theodora deposited the bike on the hard, then bethought her and pushed it out of sight in the reeds. Then she stepped on to the raft and gently pulled the rope. It moved her slowly and silently towards the boat. Her weight depressed the wooden boards but did not sink it. The price of boarding is wet feet, she thought to herself. The raft nudged up against the stern and she hauled herself over the low stage into the hold. She stopped for a moment and listened. The light had almost gone. There was nothing but the slap slap of the water against the side of the boat.

Should she risk a light? She opened the door into the cabin and climbed down the steep couple of steps. The smell of oil, bitumen and calor gas reached her nostrils. She could see very little. She fumbled her torch from her Barbour pocket and played it around. 'So,' she said to herself. 'This is where Joshua lived.'

Everything was neat. On each side were padded seats which could act as bunks. In the fore a table on a brass hinge hung down. Neat shelves were built in to the space above the bunks. They contained a range of books with titles like *A Pilot's Guide to the Waterways of England*. But on the far bunk was a bundle of clown's clothes and a cap and bells. Theodora looked round. What am I looking for? She looked at the bunks. Under each was a couple of lockers. She pulled out the port side and found blankets, a seaman's jacket and a pair of life jackets. In the starboard lockers, one held a pan and a selection of tins of ham and sardines. The other had two manila files stacked on top of each other. As her hand went for them she was aware of a beam of light other than her own penetrating the portholes on the port side. Swiftly she doused her torch and stuffed the files into the poacher's pocket of her Barbour. Then she made her way back down the cabin to a shallow recess behind the door that she guessed was usually used as a wardrobe. She gave thanks that that same instinct which had made her conceal her bicycle in the reeds had also made her close the cabin door behind her.

Lucy Royal settled herself at the corner table of her new find. One of the delights of Bolly's was there were so many odd corners which other people hadn't found where you could enter a quite different life or indeed be on your own. Lucy had found one such spot on Tuesday afternoon. On Thursday afternoon she returned to it. It was a small glass-sided room at the top of a stairway leading off the ladies' lounge of Harries Bar. To get to the stairs you had to dodge the constable sitting in the ladies' lounge which the police were using as an interview room. Lucy, long practised in getting her way in the face of far more recalcitrant officials than a country bobby, smiled kindly at him and asked him if he was cold in the heatless atmosphere. They chatted amicably for some time before she moved as if she had been doing it for many months up the staircase to the watch tower above.

From her site plan she had learned that it was called Red River Café, but there were no facilities for a café, only gilt-painted basket chairs which creaked when she sat in one and heavy 1930s-style tables. Instead she had brought their own picnic basket with its kettle and tea-making apparatus. Now she plugged it in and settled down to what she and Arthur used to call a 'brose'. A brose was halfway between a snooze and a browse. The browse could happen because of the truly splendid view over the whole camp. The room was higher than anything else around it and perched at the corner of the camp looking out towards the sea on one side and the town and the perimeter fence on the other. While she waited for the kettle to boil she made her tour of the room by walking slowly round the whole of it taking the view from each side.

The camp had been constructed, she guessed (built would be too formal a word for what had been done), in the 1950s when a holiday camp was a grand new concept and people expected little. It had degenerated steadily ever since. Buildings and expectations had swung apart. Expectations had grown as the buildings had declined. In the 1950s (Lucy could remember well, it was only the other day in her time span), the American scene had been the admired one, the Wild West the most familiar. Hence it must have seemed jaunty and original to put up a replica of Wild West Main Street with saloons and cinemas, brassy shops and eating houses all on a small and intimate scale. Now it all looked as though it was out of season by several decades. It seemed a fitting venue for a set of clergy at the end of their tether.

Lucy took up the kettle and poured water into the jug with its sprinkling of lapsang at the bottom. The smell, at once delicate and pungent, overcame the odours of dust and rotting linoleum. For a moment she regretted Arthur's absence, but he had found a crony from Kenya days and wanted to catch up. They never interfered with each other's pursuits. They were so happy when they met up again. Then she settled herself in a chair with her face towards the sea and imagined she was on a ship, one of those nice old-fashioned Channel steamers of her youth, *The Maid of Orleans* perhaps, which had carried her so often on her first ventures abroad in her teens and started her off on her love of travel. Was it a wish to see the world or a wish to spread the Word, she sometimes wondered, which had led her to the missionary life? No matter now, the love, the passion which she felt for both enterprises was with her yet. She wasn't failing whatever Arthur's gentle incredulity might imply. She knew that there was something amiss in this conference, perhaps in the Church at large. The only question was what form was it taking and who was involved? She thought again of the gossip she had heard about Adjumentum Salvatoris. Who were its members and was there any connection with the Bishop's muddled slides or indeed with the death of that poor young man Makepeace?

Lucy moved her chair nearer to the glass of the bay windows and wrapped her shawl more closely about her. She gazed down towards the area where the camp stopped and the promenade began. The razor wire was really a most unfortunate symbol, she felt. Wire had had such a bad history. She could just remember her older brothers who had served in the Great War describing to their father the business of getting through the wire. Then in the many camps she had worked in Africa how it had always seemed the last resort of the tyrant, the uncivil military, to dump coils of the stuff round inoffensive bits of land and collections of cowed people. What made it necessary to keep some people out and others in? The Church, which did a fair amount of that sort of thing, was well situated behind this particular wire.

At four o'clock the sun was almost gone. Lucy finished her tea, yawned and stretched like an old stiff Siamese cat and prepared to depart. The lights were beginning to come on over the camp and in the town. She gathered up her bag and basket and took one last look through the window.

Then she stopped and looked more carefully. Down towards the end of the wire where it met the promenade there was a patch of shadow. The shadow moved carefully but confidently through the fence, pulling the wire back a couple of feet and then edging through. Once on the other side the wire sprang back. Lucy scrabbled in her bag and extracted her bird-watchers, a delicate pair of opera glasses with ivory covers which she held on a stick. They had served her well in her long and diverse life for birds and other things; they were light to carry and powerful to use. She used to remark that her mother had seen Pavlova through them.

She adjusted the lens and followed the figure as it ran up the concrete steps on the other side of the wire. The figure was male, youngish and moved like someone who was fit. It was dressed in a black clerical suit with a short naval-type duffel thrown over. It looked to Lucy very like Father Martin Guard. So Father Guard knew a way into and out of the camp other than past the authorised entry manned by the young red-haired man, Jason was it? Well, of course, having been in the Navy he would be resourceful about such things. Lucy's first thought was that she too would like her own private door into the camp. How nice it would feel to be able to come and go as one pleased, how free and privileged. Her next thought was why should he want to have his own exit and entrance? No one else seemed inconvenienced by the more usual modes of access. Her final thought was that if Father Guard had indeed gone out, it might be a possible moment to see if she could pick up more about Adjumentum Salvatoris by taking a quick look round his chalet, which, she had discovered, was next to their own.

'So how well did you know Joshua Makepeace?'

Father Martin Guard fixed his eye on Spruce as though he were a target at the other end of a gun barrel. 'I knew him as a midshipman knows a lieutenant.'

'How well is that?'

'Lieutenants are busy making the point that they aren't midshipmen any more.'

Spruce grinned. He'd had half an hour with Jason Taint, the red-headed gatekeeper, to hear the boy's story with his own ears. Jason had revealed that his family hailed from the East End of London and had moved out in his father's time. Hence Jason spoke a fluent version of cockney overlaid with the odd tincture of East Anglian vowels. Talking to Jason was indeed like talking a foreign language, one in which there were no abstract nouns. He'd got Jason to admit that he had been late on duty on Monday evening. He rather thought his first customer had been an important old guy in a Rover, yes? Like. Why had he been late? Dunno. He'd been at The Buccaneer and sort of lost track of time, like. Had he come via the laundrette? Might have. Had he? Yes. Had he seen anything? No, he'd told them before. So, stalemate.

Questioning Martin Guard was the difference between throwing a ball at a brick wall and throwing it to someone who caught it and then refused to give it back. Spruce looked at the easy, efficient young officer turned priest. What would he get out of him?

'Did you renew your connection with Makepeace when you came into the diocese?'

'I've only been in the diocese a couple of months.'

'And you live in the Old Rectory of St Lawrence?'

'Of course. I am the incumbent of the parish.' Guard seemed amused.

'And Father Raymond Sentinel, the retired incumbent, also lives there?'

'Clearly.'

'Where were you before that?'

'I was priested two years before I came to St Lawrence's,

Wrackheath. Before that I was travelling.'

'Would that be for your missionary society, what's it called . . . ?' Spruce waited for Guard to supply the name.

'Adjumentum Salvatoris. Yes.'

'And what is the particular work of that society?'

'It has houses in different parts of the world,' said Guard distantly. 'We do in each country what the needs of the country require.'

'Where were you last?'

'I was in South America at our house just outside Caracas.'

'And was Makepeace an AS priest?'

There was a long pause. 'I'm afraid I can't reveal the membership. We keep a degree of confidentiality about named individuals.'

'May I remind you we have a murder inquiry?'

'May I remind you that the Church has a long tradition of suffering to keep the secrets of the faithful.'

Spruce felt there was a mistake here somewhere which he couldn't quite put his finger on. Surely revealing membership of a society, even a Church society, wasn't on a par with the seal of the confessional. Guard carried on as though it was a Masonic obligation. He wished he'd got Theodora beside him. Still it was likely that if he had, he'd get even less out of Martin Guard.

'Is your society a priestly one only or do you have a place for laymen?'

'The society is a body of priests but we do have laymen associates.'

'Their task being . . . ?'

'To provide the money.' Guard smiled at him.

'And how is the money provided for your activities?'

'As I say, the devotion of laymen who think our cause a good one.'

Spruce switched again. 'Do you find some of the houses

in some of the countries bring you into political conflicts?'

'We work for a Kingdom not of this world.'

'How does that work out when this world's kingdoms don't see eye to eye with your Kingdom? How do you solve those sorts of conflicts?'

'Sometimes it isn't possible to solve it. However, we are commanded to be as gentle as doves and as wise as serpents.'

Spruce sucked this one dry and then pressed on. 'Would you think it appropriate to circumvent the law of any particular country if that law was not, in your eyes, just?'

Guard had no hesitation, indeed he seemed surprised. 'But of course.'

'And did you circumvent the law in Caracas?'

'I was a very junior member of our house there.'

Spruce sighed. 'So what about the law of this country?'

Guard gazed steadily and innocently down his gun barrel.

'Have you circumvented the law in this country?'

Guard interpreted the question in his own way. 'I have only been in post at St Lawrence for two months.'

'So you said,' Spruce concluded. 'And during that time you did not come across Makepeace?'

'His reputation is, was, of course, a growing one.'

Dammit, that was not what I asked you, you casuistical young priest, Spruce did not say. 'Did you meet him on any occasion?'

'He was not part of the diocesan structures.'

'That's not what I asked.'

'No, but that's what I'm answering.' Guard wasn't offensive, just matter of fact.

That was all he was going to say.

Nick Trimming stared at his father. 'Cousin Theodora here, for dinner, tonight?'

'Be rather nice to see her again after all this time, don't you think?'

'Why?'

'Really, Nick, there's no need to be churlish. Because we're poor shall we be inhospitable? I don't imagine they do them too well down at that creaking holiday camp place. The least we can do for the poor girl is to offer her a decent supper.'

'But we haven't got a decent supper,' Nick pointed out. 'We haven't had a decent supper in ages.' They stood facing each other across the bare table of the dank kitchen at Wrackheath.

'Well, naturally there's no point in gorging ourselves when we're *en famille*. I was brought up to believe that a plain diet was a healthy diet, as Nanny used to say.'

Nick refrained from saying that a daily diet of bacon sandwiches at Laddy's supplemented by a hunk of bread and cheese in the evenings could hardly count as healthy living. He knew he could never best his father in this mood. Reality was not a factor his father wrestled with. 'What are you going to offer by way of food, then?' he asked, genuinely curious.

Randolph Trimming looked smug. 'Had a little dig in the old vegetable plot this morning,' he announced proudly.

'So?'

'Some splendid potatoes and stuff. Absolutely free from poisons. Real home-grown produce. Organic,' he said, producing the word like a mantra.

'Where?'

'I put 'em in the vegetable rack,' said Randolph, happy in his new domestic role.

Nick padded across the cold stone flags of the kitchen to the Victorian storage arrangements below the cupboard. Instinctively he glanced upwards to the top shelf. He was a head taller than his father. He caught a glimpse of the precious phone still safely in place. Then he swung back the zinc gauze of the lower cupboard. Inside was a mound of soil and some small green-looking potatoes. Beside them was a bundle of what looked like seaweed.

'What's this?' he asked, gathering up the goodies and dumping them on the table.

'Not too sure, to be honest,' his father admitted. 'Sort of Swiss chard perhaps?'

'Where'd you find it?' his son asked suspiciously.

'Went down the conservatory. It was growing on the manure we bought for the antimacassar plants.'

Nick liked the 'we'. He was not guilty of that particular crime against nature. He recalled the aspidistras wilting unhappily in the foetid air of the conservatory. He pinched a bit of the leaf and smelled the result. It was pungent and slightly peppery.

'What do you intend doing with it?'

'I thought it would go rather well lightly boiled. One should never over-cook green vegetables.' His father was didactic as though from years of gourmet living. 'With a knob of butter,' he finished triumphantly. 'Delicious. I've no doubt Theo will be very grateful.'

'Boiled potatoes and an unknown green?' Nick looked doubtful.

'Ah. But you must see my *pièce de résistance*.' His father was positively dancing now with glee. He beckoned his son towards the door. 'On the slab beside the rain butt. Have a look.'

Nick felt his way out into the dark air of the yard. The cold drizzle that threatened to turn to rain dripped down his long hair on to his thin shirt collar. To the left of the door was a rain butt into which water was steadily plopping. Beyond it a low stone slab. He thought he could remember as a boy watching a cook sitting on it in summer as she shelled peas. Beside the slab were propped his father's fishing rod and a landing net. On the slab itself was a large silver fish. Gingerly he picked it up by the tail. The thing was about two feet long and its head had the considering evil look of an old pike. Its teeth were bared, perhaps in anger at being at last caught.

'I thought for a treat,' said his father's voice over his shoulder.

Nick was admiring. 'Where'd you catch it?'

'Our own stock, of course. He's been cruising on the cocky ruff down by Keepers.'

Nick nodded. 'How d'you cook him?'

'My dear boy, everyone knows how to cook pike. It's a most delicate fish. Gut it, scale it and stuff it with herbs, then steam it.'

Nick thought all this sounded quite reasonable – for his father. 'Where would we get the herbs?'

Randolph was now not to be balked in resourcefulness. 'Some of our famous organic greens of course.'

'But then we shan't have anything to offer as a vegetable.'

'There's plenty more where that came from. I'll tootle down and restock, if you like, while you start in on the preparations.'

Theodora thought the only thing she really wanted at the moment was a hot bath and a change of clothes. She wondered whether Cousin Randolph might possibly be able to provide at least the former and if he would think it strange of her to make the request. He was, after all, family.

She had pedalled hard for over an hour, making good time over the flat roads she encountered in the later part of her journey. She had not felt safe until she gained the main Felixstowe-Highcliffe road with its comforting stream of rush-hour traffic. She wondered how the presence who had stumbled past her into the cabin of *The Pike* had coped with getting back to shore. She'd been blessed. The figure was unfamiliar with boats – or with this boat – and had missed the last step down into the cabin. She'd felt the stuff of his jacket brush her as he stumbled past and heard the crash as he hit the floor. She'd slipped out into the cockpit and was on the raft in an instant, paying out the rope to gain the reed bed. She wondered whether it was cheating to untie the rope at the other end so that there could be no possibility of whoever was on the cruiser hauling it back. She reckoned all was fair in mayhem and murder. She had, after all, no way of knowing whether their intent was innocent or not.

The road to Wrackheath was narrow, the banks on either side steep and chalky. She kept going, thinking she must be fitter than she had thought. Another ten minutes would see her there. She heard behind her the noise of a car engine attacking the incline with a change of gear. The road was narrow. Would the driver see her with Victor's small rear reflector light or ought she to pull in and let him pass? Before she could make the decision the car was on her. She was aware of a screech of brakes then the car revved on. She levered herself off the chalk bank. The damp white paste of chalk had been added to the rest of her disarray. She caught her breath. The noise of the car was receding into the distance. Thankfully she turned into Wrackheath's gates and bumped up the rutted drive.

The shallow steps up to the portico were more chipped than she remembered them from childhood. But the pleasure she had in the proportions of the whole was the same. It really was a very grand house. She looked for a bell. It was hidden and when she at last found it and pulled it there was no response. She tried again and at the third attempt there was a sound of doors closing and opening. Cousin Randolph could be seen through the glass on the other side of the door holding a torch in one hand and wrestling with the door with the other. The uneven and darting light of the torch looked like a type of early cinema or amateur theatrical performance. Bits of Randolph or the door or Theodora would suddenly be illuminated and then plunged once more into darkness. Eventually Randolph won and the door swung half open.

Randolph was arrayed in a plum-coloured velvet jacket, a whitish shirt and a dark purple bow tie. Theodora realised he had changed for dinner.

'My dear Theo,' he said and embraced her stiffly on the right cheek. 'How very kind of you to honour us. Come down to the kitchen. We're dining informally tonight. We thought you'd prefer that since we're just the family. May I take your coat? We lack servants, I'm afraid. But it puts us in touch with the real world, don't you think? The other half and so on. As a family we ought perhaps to have done it sooner. Then we might be more prosperous and could afford servants. QED. Full circle and all that.' He chuckled happy in his own logic.

He relieved Theodora of the Barbour, soaking wet and with its arm caked with chalk. She was in grey cords which were by now darkened with rain and muddy at the turn-ups. A quick appraisal of the situation suggested that this was no place to ask for a bath or a shower. They probably used the pump in the stable yard.

No one remarked on her lack of party appearance. Randolph led her through the suite of rooms which she remembered from childhood. Now as the light from his torch flashed up and down she could see how decayed they were and how beautiful. The draught from the momentarily opened door had raised a cloud of dust, creating a haze of supernatural quality in the square space. The staircase in marble and iron rose into impenetrable shadow. They made their way down the hall, turned through what must have been the old dining room where Theodora remembered a ceiling which she had gazed at long and hard as a child before understanding what the figures depicted on it were doing. Now under the eccentric illumination of her cousin's lighting arrangements she saw nothing and was aware only of the height of the room and its coldness. They passed though and out into a powder closet in the panelling of which was cut a servants' door. Then they plunged down a steep narrow staircase. Before they reached the end of it the torch gave out.

'Lead kindly light,' said Randolph inappositely. Theodora could see why Canon Hugh regarded him as no fit person to be in charge of children. She looked forward to seeing at closer quarters how Nick had turned out. Randolph opened the door into the kitchen and they stepped through.

Theodora glanced round. The kitchen was warm if dimly lit by a single electric blub hanging from the ceiling. There was a smell of boiling fish masking the prevailing smell of damp and drains. Nick was standing with his back to the room stoking the ancient cast iron range with sticks. He turned round flushed but triumphant. 'I think it's going to be all right.'

'That's a good lad,' said his father as though to a Labrador.

Theodora came forward hand outstretched. 'Nick, how very nice.'

Her cousin embraced her and she was suddenly moved by his youth and his unaffected willingness to show his feelings.

'You're very welcome. Dad and I . . .' He trailed off. 'We've got some sherry,' he said proudly.

Theodora felt that anything with alcohol in it would be welcome right now. It was tepid and very sweet like the best kind of cough mixture. She felt instantly revived by it. Outside the rain could be heard pouring into the gutter, inside all was hospitality and kindness. They swapped family news. Randolph particularly liked news of other members of the family who were failing. This was not easy to provide since Braithwaites tended in unexciting ways to be discharging their public and private duties with steady if unremarkable success. Theodora thought around amongst those of her relations of whom Canon Hugh disapproved or did not mention. She'd just pinpointed the regrettable niece of Cousin Roger drying out for the third time somewhere in California having ditched both second husband and her own two children when there was a sound of a telephone ringing. Possibly because the sound was for so long unfamiliar to him, Randolph did not show any sign of having heard it.

There was a pause and then the ringing could be heard again. Nick grasped the edge of the table as though wrestling with the inevitable, rose and dashed over to the cupboard. He scrabbled in the back of the top shelf and extracted the still ringing phone. He held it for a moment as though it were a bomb which he might hurl from himself then he pressed its buttons and clamped it to his ear. He listened intently to the thin tinkle of sound which came through the machine.

'But, Jas, I can't just now. We've got guests.'

His father gazed at him with interest. 'Jolly little things those. I've often thought perhaps the answer to our problems. Not as cumbersome as the big things we used to have plumbed in in the butler's pantry.'

'They come expensive,' Theodora thought it only fair to warn him.

'Expensive? Do they? They charge for the calls, do they?'

''Fraid so.'

Randolph appeared to lose interest. 'Come on, Nick,' he said impatiently. 'Our guest must be starving after all her exercise.' It was the only reference he had made to Theodora's bedraggled state. 'Nick.' His tone was sharp. 'Come along, dear boy.'

'Got to go, Jas.' Nick's tone was desperate. 'See you.'

'Sorry,' he said to Theodora. 'Sorry, I'll have to go out

after . . .' He gestured helplessly.

'Not before dinner,' said Randolph with a sudden burst of authority perhaps stemming from hunger. 'Afterwards, possibly.'

'Right,' said Nick. 'Right. Here we go then.' He took an ancient frayed oven cloth from the dresser and a poker in his other hand. He tapped the poker on the iron bolt of the oven door and levered it open. A gust of heat and an intensified smell of fish filled the room. Wisely Nick made no attempt to convey the fish from its kettle to a serving plate. Instead he seized the kettle with the oven cloth and conveyed it in a single tottering movement to the centre of the kitchen table. It was indeed a splendid sight. From its guts trailed a swathe of what looked like green pond weed. Its tail which had not caught the steam had rusted to a dark brown colour. Its head flopped sideways but retained even in death its expression of snarling anger. They all gazed at it in admiration.

'Jolly good,' said Randolph.

'It's not bad, is it?' Nick said with modest triumph.

'From your own pond?' Theodora knew what was expected from a guest in such circumstances.

'Had my eye on the blighter for some time,' Randolph admitted untruthfully.

Nick dived back to the oven and brought out a couple of tureens with some green-looking potatoes in one and a mound of pond weed in the other. Randolph served, shooting his cuffs and wielding an ancient-looking fish server with a yellowing ivory handle whose colour matched the teeth of the fish.

It wasn't anything like as bad at it looked. Theodora, who had the advantage of the best sauce, hunger, tucked in. The flesh was coarse and hard and tasted strongly of pond weed and some sort of peppery herb. It could have done with a bit more salt and perhaps a strong cheese sauce but if it wasn't delicious it was far from inedible. There was a pause in the conversation whilst they all got to grips. Randolph had produced a bottle of Sancerre which came from that part of the cellar which had not been sold the last time there was a financial crisis. From Theodora's view absolutely everything looked a lot better.

'I took some exercise down by Drain Dyke this afternoon,' she put in as her pennyworth of table conversation.

'Haven't been there for years,' Randolph contributed. 'Used to go frost-biting there. You can work up from the river to the broad.'

'Not now,' said Nick unexpectedly. 'They don't cut the reeds back or dredge like they used to.'

'You're very knowledgeable, old boy.'

'Got a friend who used to work in the docks and knows about boats and things.' There was pride in his voice for his friendship's sake.

'Where d'you meet him?' asked his father.

'Inside. He'd done some nicking. Not big stuff, not to deprive anyone. Mostly small stuff, like.' Theodora thought he was going to say mobile phones. But he concluded lamely: 'This and that.'

Theodora thought Nick's accent changed according to whether he was talking to and about his relations or whether he was talking about his own friends. She wondered if this meant that his mind contracted and expanded as well as his vocabulary.

'I'm not sure I approve of friends from inside.' Randolph's tone was mild, as any father with a boy at prep school warning his son about the need to make nice friends. But it was too late for Nick, wasn't it? Theodora thought. He'd not had much of an opportunity to make nice friends and now it seemed he'd met some nasty ones.

'What do you want to do, I mean, in general?' Theodora thought she might as well. After all Randolph had said 'family matters' in his invitation.

'I like engines,' Nick admitted, 'and I like the docks. They're absolutely brill.' He sounded about eleven years old. Theodora thought of Superintendent Spruce's words about him not being right in the top storey. 'But what I mostly like' – he looked apologetic – 'is here. The house. Our house.'

Theodora warmed to him.

'Jason had a job in the docks before he got put inside.' Nick was going on giving himself the pleasure of talking about his friend. 'In fact, he still dosses down there, like, when things are a bit rough at home.' He looked at his father and Theodora wondered whether Nick joined Jason when things were a bit rough at home.

'Nick is considering his options,' said his father grandly. 'And when he retires and leaves us to the port, I'd very much value your advice in that matter, you being so much closer to modern youth, ear to the ground and so on.'

Theodora, who did not consider herself close to modern youth and had no ear to any ground, refrained from denying the hopeful parent's description. Nick pushed his bones to the side of his plate, licked his fork and stacked it neatly on the other side of the plate and said pleasantly, with more social poise than he'd displayed before, 'I'll be off then. You two can settle my future for me. It'll be a great burden lifted from all our shoulders. Good night, Dad. I shan't be late. Just going round the estate.' Theodora was amused to see he pecked his father on the cheek before shaking her by the hand, unhitching his blue anorak from the peg beside the door and striding off into the night.

About the port Randolph had not been lying. He went to the dresser and took out the bottle which was about two-thirds full. It occurred to Theodora that she had had enough to drink but she thought, What the heck.

'He moves between being quite grown up and being really

rather young,' Theodora ventured.

'I wish his mother had stayed a bit longer,' Randolph said. Theodora thought this didn't help things along. What Nick needed was meaningful work, skills, a trade.

Randolph was maundering on. 'What in fact I was wondering was, I mean, Nick needs to get away from here. Wider world. Bit more experience. He's got some crack-brained scheme for putting this lot to rights.' He waved his hand in the direction of the house above him. 'And, of course, he can't do it. We none of us can. Does he really think I haven't tried? What could he do that I have not already done?'

Theodora thought there was resentment there but also common sense.

'What sort of scheme?'

Randolph considered this before answering, then he seemed to feel that if he was going to get anything to his advantage from Theodora he would need to come clean. 'At the moment his idea seems to be to take in lodgers.'

Theodora thought of all that she had seen so far of the creature comforts of the house. 'And has that been successful?'

'Haven't seen a penny.' Randolph sounded aggrieved.

'How many and who?' Theodora was genuinely curious.

'Haven't a clue.'

Surely this was rather odd even for someone with Randolph's capacity for screening out the real world.

'When did they start?'

'We've only had one lot so far. They came last month. I'm not too sure who they were. They came at night and spent a night here and then went on very early in the morning. I can't say I thought much of their transport. It was a sort of horse-box affair.'

Theodora was beginning to suspect Randolph was playing games. 'But you must have met them. Bed and breakfasters would expect to meet the host, wouldn't they?'

Randolph took this on as a new idea. 'Of course, you're quite right. I never thought of that. Why didn't he introduce us? I expect he thought they weren't up to my standards. Anyway, he's kept the whole thing to himself. Not a word to me.' He pushed his plate of pike bones away, refilled his port glass and passed it to Theodora. She wondered if she should, decided against it, then refilled her glass.

'Where did they stay, I mean which rooms?'

'Funny you should ask that. I would have thought the old north view rooms, the Blue Lady's room and Uncle Matthew's, would just about be habitable.' Randolph was unwontedly honest.

'But he didn't put them there?'

'No. He put them in the maids' rooms in the attic.'

'How do you know?'

Randolph sniggered. 'Went and had a shufti round when he was out with the appalling Jason one day.'

'And?'

'Traces of food. Not my kind of stuff. All this modern pasta and beans. Mineral water too.' He sipped his port and expressed his distaste. 'And they all sleep under duvets now, I understand. Most unhygienic.'

Theodora, a duvet woman herself and not above a dish of pasta if offered, reserved judgement.

'What if we were to go up and see the accommodation?' Randolph said, greatly daring. 'Then you could give me your considered opinion about the future profitability of my son's venture.'

Theodora saw he was drunk. She stood up and realised she was not what her father would have called impeccable herself. She held on to the end of the table and said, forming her words with care, 'Lay on, MacDuff.' The phrase came to her in Uncle Hugh's diction.

Randolph dispensed with the pretence that there was

any electric light anywhere else in the building. He took a brass candle holder from the dresser and started up the servants' staircase.

CHAPTER NINE

Blood Brothers

'Tibor? Where?'

Spruce put the phone to his ear more tightly and wrote on his pad. 'Wrackheath Hall. Yes, yes I know where it is. This line's very bad. It isn't Theodora Braithwaite, is it? Oh, it is. Theo. Where have you found Tibor? At Wrackheath Hall. What's he doing there? OK.' He looked at his watch. It said half past ten. 'OK, I'll send someone immediately to pick him up and I'll be up myself in twenty minutes. Are you all right? Fine. And, Theo, pretty good, I'd say.'

'More luck than any ability in detection, I have to admit,' Theodora said as she met Spruce on the grand steps of Wrackheath half an hour later. The scene was lit up with blue revolving roof lights on the two police cars. A speechless and whimpering Tibor had been taken down from the attics, asking only that his tablets should be allowed to accompany him. A suspicious constable had pocketed them muttering about illegal substances and Tibor's cries of digitalis had gone unheeded.

Cousin Randolph, Theodora noticed, was much elated by the whole affair. The idea that he would resent his home being invaded by the polloi was quite wrong. He would have offered round, if not the port, at least the sherry, if Theodora had not deterred him. Of Nick there was no sign.

'I'll have to have a word or two with you, sir,' Spruce said to Randolph.

'Come into the kitchen, officer, it's cosier. You don't mind if my cousin joins us, I imagine.'

They trooped round the back of the house and entered by the kitchen door.

'So, how long has Tibor been in your attic, Sir Randolph?'

'It's a good question, Superintendent.' Randolph was clearly prepared to make a night of it. 'You see it's my son, Nick, who looks after that side of our enterprises. He has this romantic idea of restoring the family fortunes.' Sir Randolph smiled at Spruce, man of experience mocking the aspiration of naïve youth.

'What enterprise would that be?' Spruce was quite prepared to play the simple country bobby to the county landowner if that was what the latter wanted. Theodora was surprised he didn't lick his Biro before he wrote down the silly nonsense of Randolph's answer.

'We're starting up a kind of staging post, a sort of hotel, well, more a lodging house for those wanting a quick overnight stay. I suppose Tibor was really one of our earliest customers.'

Theodora grinned to herself.

'So where do they sleep, these lodgers?'

'I think Nick felt they would be more comfortable in the attics. Very nice and dry, and *warm*,' he added with emphasis. 'Heat rises, you know.'

Spruce didn't doubt it. 'Who else have you had here, do you know?'

A sly look crossed Cousin Randolph's face. 'I think we've had one or two gentlemen of colour in our time.'

'When?' Spruce was implacable.

'A couple of days ago.' Anyone else would have had the

tact not to push it, Randolph indicated.

'Who were they?'

'Again I'd have to refer you to my son.'

'You do know, sir, that keeping a hotel or indeed lodgings requires a licence from the local authority; that there are a number of health and safety regulations, including fire regulations in particular, which apply to all premises used by clients?'

'Ah, but you see, we didn't *charge* them.' Randolph was clearly entranced by his logic. He beamed across at the policeman. 'In fact, I was saying to Theo earlier this evening that I haven't seen a penny. Didn't I say so, my dear?'

Theodora had to admit that that was so.

'So you see,' Randolph was triumphant, 'they were more by way of being family friends than clients or customers or whatever.'

'But you never actually met any of them?' Spruce made no attempt to keep the incredulity out of his voice.

'You've got it in one, Superintendent.' Randolph beamed his good humour towards Spruce.

'So to find out who came and when I'd have to talk to Nick?'

'Quite right.'

'Where is he?'

'Ah, that I'm not absolutely sure about. He went out earlier in the evening to take a bit of a constitutional.'

Theodora felt that no one had taken a constitutional since 1920.

'He first received a phone call,' she volunteered.

'Who from?' Spruce turned his attention in her direction as possibly the only hope of sanity in the household.

'He didn't say,' said his father swiftly, 'and of course we couldn't inquire.'

He winked warningly at Theodora but she had had enough of wasting Spruce's time.

'He addressed his interlocutor as Jas,' she said carefully. 'I don't know if you could put a name to that.'

'Jason Taint. He's not unknown to us. Is he a close friend of your son's, Sir Randolph?'

Randolph looked distant. 'I really couldn't say.'

'Well, when is he coming back?'

'Oh, you know how these young men are, Superintendent, a law unto themselves nowadays. You can't keep a nineteen-year-old on a leading rein, can you?'

Spruce didn't vouchsafe an opinion on this.

'Of course there are other people who might be able to help you in the matter of lodgers.'

Theodora glanced at him. What was the disingenuous old beggar going to hand out next?

'And who would that be?'

'Our near neighbours and good friends the Holy Fathers down the road. They sometimes took our overspill, I believe.'

Theodora felt it had been a long day and that she probably wasn't hearing things right.

'Who?' asked Spruce. Clearly he shared Theodora's amazement.

'The good Fathers in the old vicarage, Father Raymond Sentinel and the new one, the parish priest, Father Martin, is his name Guard?'

'How do you know all this, sir?'

'Seen the van. I'm sure it's the same one parked there as comes round here. They parked it round the back on at least one occasion.'

'When?'

'Oh, I don't know. Some days ago.'

'And previously?'

'At my age one's days merge into each other, so little to stimulate round here,' Randolph said alertly.

He can't be more than fifty-five, Theodora thought, and he's certainly found a stimulating hobby spying on his neighbours and keeping track of his son's activities beyond what she would have supposed.

Spruce appeared to have come to the end of his inquiries or his tether. 'I shall need a statement from you later, Sir Randolph. For tonight I'm going to leave a man here. If your son should return, I'd like to hear from him immediately.'

'Of course, Inspector, I quite understand. I'll see to it. Civic duty and all that. Sure I can't press you to another sherry?' He indicated his own port glass. Spruce, who had taken nothing, looked a little baffled. 'Well, goodnight, Sergeant. May I wish you every fortune in your inquiries? And please be assured that I am at all times entirely at your service. My hobby is fishing, you see.'

Theodora thought this was quite a bravura performance and said so as she walked down the drive with Spruce to his car. If she had been Spruce with a murder on his hands she would have been angry but it was clear that Spruce was adding Sir Randolph to his collector's gallery of social eccentrics.

'Quite a chap, your uncle,' he said appreciatively.

'Cousin,' said Theodora dourly. 'And he's telling a pack of lies. Nick has been harbouring people in the attic and his father was not informed.'

'So I would surmise.' Spruce was judicious. 'So where is he now?'

'I don't know but if Jason is that young redhead on the gate I do hope Nick's not too deeply involved with him.'

'We saw them the other night, Tuesday if you remember, at The Buccaneer.'

Theodora nodded. 'With the van, yes.' She turned to Spruce in real anxiety. 'What is going on?'

'You tell me. It's your cousin.'

'Are you going to question the two priests now?'

Spruce looked at his watch. 'I think we should all be a

lot fresher in the morning. I fancy from what we've seen of Father Martin so far, we'll need all our wits about us. Can I give you a lift back to Bolly's?'

Theodora thought of her or rather Victor's bike still on the steps of the house. 'I've got a bicycle,' she said.

'Put it in the back of the Rover,' Spruce said looking at her tired face in the dim light of his car lamp. 'You look all in.'

'I've had a lot of exercise today,' she admitted. She felt the bulk of the two files purloined from *The Pike* in the pocket of her Barbour. It was on the tip of her tongue to say I've found where the jester priest hung out and I've got some of his records. But the moment passed.

'I'd love a lift,' she said gratefully.

'. . . proclaim the mysteries of Faith,' intoned Father Sentinel.

'Christ has died, Christ is risen, Christ will come again,' shouted his congregation of thirty crammed without elbow room into the chapel next to the laundrette at the seventhirty a.m. mass on Friday. Father Martin Guard and Canon Oldsalmon and Father Sentinel moved decorously around each other in the cramped space of the tiny sanctuary. Ten minutes later they were all done and dusted. Priests and congregation streamed forth in the direction of breakfast, their appetites sharpened by the early start and the feeling of religious duties properly performed. It was a fine November morning with a strong cold sun streaming from the east and blinding them as they came round the corner from the chapel. In Main Street were a number of cars which did not look like clergy ones. A marked police car with a woman police officer chatting to a male police officer was parked outside Harries Bar. They were not high enough up in the hierarchy to make them feel involved in the crime. Meanwhile Joshua Makepeace was still unavenged and those responsible for his murder walked free.

Lucy Royal detached herself from the arm of her husband and padded after Theodora a little ahead of her in the crowd.

'Arthur doesn't believe me,' she said, 'so you're the only person I can turn to.' Lucy made it sound like an honour, which in a way it was.

'How can I do that?' Theodora had reflections of her own to attend to. She'd got up at five to study the files from *The Pike*. She needed to think about what to do next, what indeed to tell Spruce. She had no intention of holding out on him but she intended to have more of the case before her before handing it over. Indeed, given the delicate relationships in the Church she wondered whether he would understand what was happening. She looked down from her height to the tiny composed figure of Lucy Royal trotting beside her.

'It's about' – Lucy lowered her voice – 'it's about A S.'

'Yes,' said Theodora. For a moment she was touched by guilt. She should have reported back to Lucy before. It was just that she'd had other things happening to her. 'Yes, I did have a word with my contact, with Gilbert Racy, about Adjumentum Salvatoris. It's—'

'I know all about Adjumentum Salvatoris.' Lucy seemed to feel this would be a matter of surprise to Theodora. Theodora, having just read the files from *The Pike*, wondered if this could be true.

'What about them?'

'They're everywhere.'

'Is that a bad thing?'

Lucy considered this apparently dispassionately. 'In some ways no, in some ways yes. They are certainly faithful priests, altar and office men.'

'Rare enough nowadays.'

'How very true. But . . .'

175

'But what?' Theodora was getting tired of these pussyfootings. She had serious work to do.

'It's the secrecy, the exclusiveness. And now the plot.'

'Secrecy, I'll give you; exclusiveness, often happens in male society. "Who can we keep out?" type thing. Plot though, I don't follow. What plot?'

Lucy took her arm and steered her with its surprisingly powerful grip down Main Street and in the direction of the chalets. Theodora, her mind on breakfast, allowed herself to be led with reluctance.

'It has a plan to take over the Church. I had a look at the membership list. The whole world is in it.'

'How do you mean?' Theodora was momentarily distracted. Ahead she could see Jason Taint, the redhaired security guard, in conversation with a uniformed policeman. Jason did not look too happy about the exchange.

'Theo, dear, you are not attending. I said I got hold of a membership list of Adjumentum Salvatoris.'

Theodora didn't seem to take the point.

'It's a *secret* society. It's not supposed to let its membership be known.'

'So? How did you get a list?'

Lucy looked both furtive and triumphant. 'I burgled Father Martin Guard's chalet last evening. He's in the one next door to us. It wasn't terribly difficult. They are terribly flimsy. A good kick.'

'Good gracious,' Theodora allowed herself. 'Whatever made you go to such lengths?'

'I was having tea yesterday afternoon in my little eyrie, that watch tower above Harries Bar. You really must join me sometime, it's so pleasant. Well, it had just gone dark when I saw Father Martin go through the wire.'

'Which wire? How?' Theodora was genuinely interested.

'He'd clearly been that way before. The wire of the perimeter fence just where it joins the promenade. I thought he was into something when I heard his voice the other night or morning.'

'What did you hear?'

'I told you. I heard the sound of an engine and then the sound of Umundese being spoken and then Father Martin's voice urging them to be quick.'

'Ah, yes,' Theodora said. 'About the Umundese. I did actually ring the legation. They were quite sure that there were none of their people in Highcliffe. The man's words were, "All our people are very very happy under our new leader. No one wishes to leave our country."'

Lucy snorted. 'I heard Umundese being spoken and Father Martin Guard, a leading light in A S, walks through the camp wire as though it didn't exist.'

Theodora reflected on all this. Twenty-four hours ago she would have dismissed it, as Arthur had, as the maunderings of an old woman who did not sleep too well and who remembered her glory days in the mission field of Africa. Now she wondered. 'So what do you think is afoot?'

'I honestly don't know. But I thought one thing we could do was to look at the list of members and see if we saw any pattern in them. And . . .'

'And?'

'Well, there is an Adjumentum Salvatoris house at Felixstowe. I wondered if we might pay it a visit. See if anything gave?'

Theodora considered. In the light of her own interests that might not be such a hare-brained scheme. 'How about some breakfast?' she suggested. 'Then we could have a look at the list, then perhaps plan the day.'

'Get him a cup of tea,' Spruce said wearily, turning round in his chair to the attentive but tired Tilby behind him.

'No, no,' said Tibor as though resisting the administration of poison. 'I drink maté, only maté.'

'And where would we find that on a bright November day?' Clearly Spruce was tired. He'd been at work since six and now he and Tilby had questioned Tibor for an hour. Neither was entirely convinced that he was Joshua Makepeace's murderer. There was time and place and circumstantial evidence but there was no motive, no connection other than the mysterious photograph in Tibor's wallet.

'I keep some in my kitchen. In the shelf at the end next to cereal packet.'

'Oh, all right. Jon, get someone to go and get it. What do you have to do with it then?'

'Just add hot water, hot not boiling,' said Tibor meekly.

The big man did not look in good shape. He might have lost a pound or two recently. He was sweating, though Heaven knew Harries Bar was not warm. He seemed to have a number of boils on his neck. Tibor's English, Spruce noticed, came and went with his willingness to answer questions. He no longer denied that he had left the kitchen on the night of the killing of Joshua Makepeace at the time when the murder was being committed between six-thirty and seven p.m. He'd gone, he said, for a mouthful of air and had walked down to the perimeter fence. He persisted that he had been nowhere near the laundrette and that he had no knowledge of or acquaintance with anyone called Joshua Makepeace.

Spruce looked at his list. He'd need to go over the question of the knife and the coat, the reason for Tibor's leaving his digs and his job and the question of visas and passports. If he couldn't get him for murder he might just get him as an illegal immigrant.

Tilby reappeared with three cups and gave the pale green brew to Tibor.

'Jon,' Spruce said, 'if you're going to Wakefield to see our friend, you'd better get started.'

Tilby nodded.

'But just before you do . . .' Spruce paused and turned to Tibor. 'Do you happen to know anyone called George Allbright?'

Tibor stopped sipping his herbal brew. It seemed to Spruce that he was considering how to reply. Tilby held his breath.

'He keeps fish and chip shop in high street. Yes, I know him well.'

'No,' said Spruce as Tilby let out his breath. 'No, he doesn't.' He nodded at Tilby. 'OK, Jon, give me a ring as soon as you know.'

'Right.' Tilby did not disguise his disappointment. 'And this has just come in.'

Spruce looked at the faxed note. It read, 'Blood on knife and jacket rhesus negative A. Makepeace was rhesus negative B. Prints on knife belonged to Tibor Makiewicz.' Spruce sighed.

Spruce took the photograph of Joshua Makepeace from its police-numbered cellophane and pushed it across to Tibor. 'This was found in your wallet in the pocket of your coat. Why were you carrying about the photograph of someone whom you say you never met and whom you have no relations with?'

Tibor gazed at the photograph. 'Ah, yes,' he said. 'He is my saviour. I carry him always with me and he brings me nothing except good luck.'

'How is he your saviour?'

Tibor licked the maté cup and ran his hand round his boils. 'When I came out of Turkey I had a bad time. I had a bad time in Turkey too, of course. Many Christians have bad time in Turkey.'

Spruce reviewed his personal encyclopaedia. 'Turkey is an Islamic country and you are a Christian,' he finally clarified.

''S right,' Tibor said. 'My mother was a good convent girl. When my father died, (he was very, very good cook, he was sous-chef at The Divan in Istanbul) she went back to her people in Hungary and she educated me properly. So far as she could. She hoped to get to America. Every one of my relations hoped to get to America. No one made it yet. But I do best. At least I get halfway. Here.' He gestured around him.

'So how did you get here?'

'I tell you. The Fathers help me.'

'Which fathers?'

'Adjumentum Salvatoris.'

'Could you spell that for me?' Spruce asked.

'No,' said Tibor. 'No, I don't think so. But it spells as it sounds.'

'So how did you get in touch?'

'I got into some trouble. Not so much, not so serious. But it is not difficult to get into trouble in Hungary. I said a bit against the government. You understand this was all before the wall came down.'

Spruce nodded. 'Go on.'

'When I was released, there were these people. They contacted many sorts who came out of prison. They do what they say pastoral work amongst the released. They were Catholics, Lutherans, Pentecostalist. I had hoped for Pentecostalist because they have contacts with America but the English Catholics got me. Or I got them.'

'And they brought you over here?'

'Round about.' Tibor was cautious. 'They take me to Holland. They get passport and visa and all that.'

'How did they bring you in?'

'I came in on *The Admiral Hardy*. It was a fine boat.'

'At dead of night, doubtless. To Felixstowe.'

'No, it was midday. All was above the table. We go through Immigration. I had the papers.' There was pride in his voice.

'So you came in in the regular way through Customs.'

'Of course. I am not a beggar. I have my skills in cooking.'

'Of course,' Spruce soothed. 'So how about the photograph of Makepeace in your wallet?'

'Who?'

'Makepeace is the name of the man whose photograph you had in your wallet. He has been unlawfully killed. Murdered. I am investigating his murder.' Spruce was patient.

'Ah, so. I did not know his name. I got photograph by the priest who met me in Hungary. He said that I should look out for him in Hevenningen at the railway as it meets the port. Under the clock.'

'And did you?'

'No. Him I never see. It was another man who touched my arm. But I kept the picture in case of need. He was the author of my release.' This didn't sound like a phrase of Tibor's own but clearly he got about a bit in the matter of language acquisition.

'What was his name? The name of the man who "touched your arm"?'

'He did not offer it,' said Tibor with dignity. 'One does not in such circumstances inquire.'

'What did he look like? How old was he? Tell me all you can about him.' Spruce was desperate.

'He was forties, fat, light brown hair, not much of it. He sweated a lot. Like me.'

'And the photograph?' Spruce pursued.

'I showed it to him. He recognised it on the spot and he did the rest.'

'He sailed the boat, *The Admiral Hardy*, across the Channel?'

'He came with us, yes. But the sailing was done by younger man. He knew a lot about ships.'

'Describe him,' Spruce said carefully.

'Dark-haired, six feet. He was athlete. What more can I say?'

'Have you ever seen him since?'

'No.'

'Have you ever seen the fat man since?'

Tibor looked furtive, then gazed straight into Spruce's eyes. 'I don't think so.'

'You don't think so?'

'When I had to leave in a hurry on Wednesday morning when you ask questions of me the first time . . .' Tibor trailed off.

'Yes, well, why did you leave your work and clear off?'

'I was told to,' Tibor said simply.

'And the fat man told you to?'

'No. But I get this message.'

'From whom and when?'

'The boy on the gate, he come with message. About half-eight. He tell me to get out quick, the police would arrest me if I don't.'

'Why should we arrest you?'

'Why not? I have been arrested before. Police do not need a reason for arrest. I spent two years in Hungary jail. They don't need reason. They just arrest.'

Spruce saw his point. 'What about your coat? Why did you leave it behind?'

'The message say, go now or else.'

'So you left your coat where?'

'I left it where it always. On the back of the door in the kitchen.'

'And the knife?'

Tibor shook his head. 'I cut myself in my hurry with meat knife.'

Spruce sighed. 'You left here at eight-thirty, Wednesday morning. You did not reach your digs until ten-thirty. You live twenty minutes' walk from here. Where were you during that time?'

Tibor looked virtuous. 'I go to doctor.'

'Why?'

'I have needs, medical needs. I have heart.' He clapped both hands to where the organ might be situated.

'Which doctor?'

'Doctor MacGuire. He is very good doctor. He understands my condition. He is interested in boils too,' Tibor said with satisfaction.

'So then you went back to your digs. What then?'

'They sent a car to fetch me.'

Spruce felt this was not the first time in twenty-four hours he had to battle with a witness whose presuppositions were not his own. 'Who sent a car and where did they take you?'

'It was a large, grey, German car. A Merc. Very comfortable. A young man drive. Thin, dark hair, twenty maybe,' he added to forestall Spruce's inquiry. He felt he was getting the hang of the rules of the game now. 'He say nothing – no, not a word – but he drive me to the house of safety up the hill. It was a very nice attic. I have known very many much worse attics and cellars,' he added by way of afterthought. 'He was very kind. He take me in round the back.'

'So who arranged all this?'

'Who but the Fathers?' Tibor seemed surprised at the question. 'They have been my help since prison the first time.'

Lucy leaned back in the luxury of Arthur's Vauxhall. Theodora drove it cautiously, as one does with other people's vehicles. 'It's very kind of Arthur to let me drive his new car.'

'I'm sure he trusts you quite as much as I do,' said Lucy complacently.

Hell's teeth, Theodora thought. She hasn't asked his

permission. She slowed down.

Through the morning they had both dutifully attended the conference's lecture and work groups. The Bishop had led with a powerful piece about starting from scratch in liturgy in order to break the incomprehension barrier of guess who, young people, at this Millennium time. As Lucy said, why not teach the young people what the liturgy means rather than rewriting the liturgy every time young people don't understand it. 'Certainly the Orthodox don't seem to be compromising in that way,' was Theodora's murmured comment to Canon Oldsalmon. 'What price Old High Slavonic?' he'd agreed.

However, at coffee the general tide was against them with talk of 'unisex, non-gender-specific texts' and prayers full of particularised, politicised and politically correct petitions just in case the Almighty was a bit old fashioned and hadn't yet caught up with what was expected of Him. 'We want,' said Chris Teane to an interested group, 'prayers that are on message.'

'Whose message?' Lucy had inquired. But she wasn't young enough to warrant a reply.

'So who are the members of Adjumentum Salvatoris?' Theodora asked as she negotiated the roundabout and struck up country from The Buccaneer.

'I can tell you one person who isn't and that's Canon Oldsalmon.'

'Why is that surprising?'

'Well, he's Forward in Faith and fairly uncompromising.'

'Principled.'

'If you like.'

'So Forward in Faith doesn't equal AS.'

'No. It has to do with mission and politics.' Lucy fumbled in her capacious bag and drew out a prayer-book-sized volume with black covers. It had nothing written on the outside. She flicked through the pages.

Towards the back, she began to read out, 'Makepeace, Sentinel, Bloomfield—'

'Bloomfield? But he's not a priest.'

'There are quite a lot of laymen. All rather distinguished. Sir Henry Vallens. Do you know him? He was something frightfully grand, ambassador to this, that and t'other. Arthur was at school with him. Arthur would never criticise an old school friend, especially one from the same house,' she remarked inconsequentially. 'In fact what you notice is that wherever AS has a house they also have the names of diplomatic staff – some, as I say, highly placed.'

'How's it arranged?'

'There's a full list, at least I assume it's full, first of priests then of laymen. No addresses or phone numbers, which is rather vexing.'

'Then?'

'Then there's a section called "provinciae".'

'Spheres of operation,' Theodora said.

'How I wish I had the learned tongues,' said Lucy.

Theodora, who had, said, 'It's useful as a basis when dealing with people like AS. I do wonder, though, why they hark back to the Latin when their pattern, which is clearly the Roman Church, has thrown it all out.'

'Oh, do you think it has?' Lucy said. 'I always feel it's there all the time just lurking below the surface. Like that pond weed which dies if it comes up.'

She'd lost Theodora who said, 'Which way now?'

Lucy looked at the map. 'I'm afraid it's a long hack through the suburbs. The house is called St Ignatius and St Martin.'

'Lot of soldiers there,' said Theodora.

'And it's in Acacia Avenue off Chestnut Drive.'

Theodora got the picture. 'Go on about how the Book of the Society is arranged.'

'Well, as I say, the world – and I mean the whole world, they've got us all in one province or another – the world is

185

divided into provinces and they've got a name of a house in each province and the names of the priests and laymen attached to each. Marked absence of women from the lay list.'

'So whose province are we in?'

'Eastern England. There's a map. It runs from Peterborough to Deal. And each area has what they call a *dominus*. Our *dominus* is Raymond Sentinel. The house is the thing we're heading for. And our layman is Kenneth Bloomfield.'

'Nice and symmetrical,' said Theodora. 'I wonder where they meet o' nights. Do go on.'

'Well, as you see, it's terribly boys gamesish. They have grades and levels and there are a lot of stars and crosses and things to represent years of seniority and a grade key. You get the picture.'

Theodora got the picture. She felt suddenly tired. Why did men do this sort of thing and women not? Was it just a hangover from the public schools from the nineteenth century or had they always done it? She thought of the origins of Wrackheath and her ancestor, the Hell-fire Club Trimming, who had built it. What had the society been but a magic equivalent of AS?

'So can we gather what they do with all these tranklements? I mean, if they have enough energy to spare after they got all their grades and have kept all the other undesirables out.'

'That's the most interesting bit,' said Lucy. 'Yes I think I can say they do a bit of good or anyway they aim to. But the difficulty is that they seem to be set on the politics of the thing. The bit on the aims of the Society at the beginning' – Lucy licked her thumb and riffled back though the pages – 'starts with a quotation from Scripture: Deuteronomy 10. 19. "Love ye therefore the stranger: for ye were strangers in the land of Egypt."'

'Nothing wrong with that,' Theodora agreed. 'Then what?'

'"Each member of our brotherhood dedicates himself to further the Kingdom by ministering to all those of the Christian Faith who are aliens and strangers. The funds of our society will be used to find and succour all such."' Lucy paused. 'It's rather grand, isn't it?'

'So Martin Guard and presumably Joshua Makepeace were dedicated to that ministry.'

'I wonder if the Umundis I heard Father Guard with the other night were aliens and strangers?'

'Ancient term for the modern political refugees. I suppose he stows them in the attics of Wrackheath?' Theodora said and filled Lucy in on the events there of the previous night.

'What about funds?' Lucy said when Theodora had finished her tale. 'It must cost a rare old packet to finance all their activities. And on the whole mission work is not well funded.' Lucy had run so many enterprises in her time that reading a balance sheet and organising the fundraising were second nature to her.

'You sound envious,' Theodora said without thinking.

'Oh, but I am. I have such difficulty getting people to help with my "Africa First" project. If we could just tap into someone with a pot of money and a really efficient organisation . . .'

Theodora thought, That's it. That's why Lucy is so interested in following up AS. They are well organised and financed. She wants a share for her own enterprises.

'Well,' said Theodora, 'perhaps we might pick up an idea or two from this lot.'

The car had entered a long row of turn-of-the-century villas in a chestnut-lined avenue. The verges were mown and the mature privet hedges of most houses were neatly trimmed. It was bin day and the wheely bins lined the side of the path like sentries in boxes. Here and there a house stuck out as having sunk a class. There the drives were unraked, the laurels run to seed, the solid Edwardian woodwork on doors and windows peeling. But they were built to last, these houses, they would take a long time to decay.

The house of St Ignatius and St Martin was not easily detected. There was no noticeboard but Lucy, flourishing a pair of opera glasses about the same date as the houses, spotted a very discreet metal plaque fixed to the door of one of the largest.

'What's our cover story?' Lucy asked, tucking her opera glasses into her bag and entering into the spirit of the enterprise.

'I have given that some thought,' Theodora replied in scholarly fashion. 'It occurred to me that it would not be too far from the truth to say that I knew Joshua Makepeace's father and he asked me to see if there were any of his son's possessions to be collected.'

'Brilliant,' said Lucy appreciatively.

They rang the bell and waited. Both the women were used to the ways of religious houses. Neither expected a swift response. After ten minutes Lucy said, 'How about going round the back?'

The garden at the rear of the house was surprisingly large. There was an expanse of lawn with a statue of the Virgin in the centre in concrete. At the far end was a life-sized crucifix. Beyond was a grotto which might have contained a pool or a fountain, now dry. Further on was a path which led to a pergola and walk. Backing and enclosing all was a shrubbery and to the left could be glimpsed a greenhouse. The place had an air of long-established peace. It was hard to imagine this was the centre of anything more exciting than religious retreats.

'The back door?' suggested Lucy.

The back door was as fast shut as the front. Lucy teetered round to the window of the main room.

'Rather what you'd expect, leather chairs, mats with holes. Looks like the dentist's waiting room of my youth. They're different now, all glass and plastic with fish.'

'No fish?'

'No, nothing.'

'How about the greenhouse?'

They walked down the gravel path and approached the door. Before they could knock, it was flung open. An immense young man, six foot and broad in proportion, with a mane of dark hair, dressed in a leather apron and jeans said, 'This is private property. No one can't come in.'

Where have I heard that before, Theodora wondered. She left it to Lucy.

'Good afternoon. I'm so glad we found someone. We were beginning to feel rather lost. We've come on an errand of mercy. You'll have heard of the sad death of Father Makepeace?'

This had the desired effect. The youth nodded.

'We've come from his father, Mr . . .' She turned to Theodora.

'Captain Henry Makepeace,' Theodora dutifully supplied.

'Of course, Captain Henry Makepeace. He has asked us to be so kind as to collect Father Joshua's belongings. Can you possibly help us?'

The young man seemed uncertain. Finally he said, 'All fathers gone. Not back till weekend.'

'That's quite all right. We wouldn't want to trouble them. I did say to Father Guard, Father Martin, we didn't expect to see anyone.'

'Father Martin,' said the reluctant youth. It seemed to release the spring. 'Follow. I show.'

He wiped his hands on a piece of towelling in his apron pocket and set off at a cracking lope across the lawn to the back door. There he produced a key of ecclesiastical proportions and beckoned them inside. He did not pause but rushed them through the kitchen. On the wall was a set of bells still labelled with rooms. The paint was green and cream and flaking. The youth hustled them into the hall of the house. Nothing had been done to it since the first set of decorations in 1900. There was lincrusta wallpaper, its embossed pattern almost obliterated by paint. Dadoes and picture rails were picked out in dark brown. They go back to the foundations of time, Theodora thought, remembering her own childhood in north Oxford vicarages and, later, south of England prep schools.

Once in the hall the youth pulled up. 'There.' He gestured. 'The third door you will find Father Joshua. May he rest in peace.' He crossed himself with a tremendous gesture across the broad bulk of his figure. The two women found themselves joining in.

Lucy put a grandmotherly hand on his arm. 'You have really been very helpful and kind. May God bless you.'

'Amen,' replied the well-schooled young man. Then he turned smartly on his heel as though from some recent drill exercise and left at the double.

'Isn't this exciting?' Lucy said and spryly began to mount the stairs.

CHAPTER TEN

Ticks and Crosses

Theodora repressed an instinct to knock. The door was not locked and she and Lucy slid in silent as serpents. Their joint gaze took in a single truckle bed, a chest of drawers and a crucifix on the wall opposite the bed. Theodora recognised it as the one in the picture in Tibor's wallet. On a hanger on the back of the door was a cassock, green with age.

'Do you think we ought to take it?'

'I doubt if Captain Makepeace will want to remember his son by it.'

'How about the chest of drawers?'

Lucy rattled the top drawer open. There was a collection of black clerical shirts and black clerical socks. On the table beside the bed was another copy of the Society's handbook which Lucy had found in Martin Guard's chalet. Theodora felt a revulsion about riffling through the dead man's possessions. She'd done this before. Nothing personal had been found on that occasion on the boat but here it was more intimate. She'd no reason to suppose this peripatetic jester had spent more time here than in other of his camps but still she did not want to intrude. He'd led a life and carried on a ministry that was entirely public. It was as if he did not want to have a private sphere other than such as to feed his basic needs. She wondered for a moment where the chapel would be in the house and how often Adjumentum Salvatoris met and worshipped together. Had the Society been for him, his family, his private life outside the world of his jesting? Was it here from this milieu that his death had come?

But however much he'd wanted to keep himself private and uncluttered by the ordinary baggage of life, she needed to have whatever information the room could provide. Lucy was continuing her progress down the chest of drawers. Theodora was aware that she had stopped. She'd reached the bottom drawer.

'Three sets of boots,' said Lucy. 'Isn't that rather a lot, given he wasn't rich or dressy? And they're the wrong colour for a priest.'

Theodora looked over her shoulder. The boots were brown and handsome on the pattern of jodhpur boots. She thought back over the cases she had been involved in over the last ten years. They reminded her of something. She extracted one and fiddled with the heel, then produced her Swiss army knife from her jacket pocket and applied it to the screws in the heel. This time they did not yield. She looked at the boots carefully. They were larger than she would have supposed for a man of Joshua's height. She weighed them in her hand: they were heavier too. She tapped them on the top of the drawers and the ring of something solid came back to her.

'Try the caps,' said Lucy.

Theodora fumbled her hand down the neck of the boot and edged it towards the toe.

'Yes,' she said, 'you're right. It's got a metal cavity insulated from the main shoe.'

'We'd better take them.' Lucy was businesslike. She

produced a polythene bag and began to stuff the boots into them.

'What would he want three pairs of brown boots with hollow toe caps for?' Theodora asked. 'Would they be part of the paraphernalia of his jesting?'

But there was no time for speculation. In the hall below could be heard voices. Theodora tiptoed to the door and looked over the stairwell. She saw a large fat man dressed in a shiny blue suit arguing with the giant from the greenhouse. There was acrimony. The name 'Makepeace' came up the stairwell. The man sounded like a bailiff, practised in getting his own way. Theodora motioned Lucy from the chest and put her fingers to her lips. Lucy slipped into action. She pointed down the corridor.

Silently the two women padded down the corridor and made for the servants' stairs at the other end. Theodora caught the scent of danger as pungent and unmistakable as a bonfire. She looked anxiously at Lucy. The old woman showed no sign of flagging. They raced down the stairs. At the bottom was a door through the glass panels of which could be glimpsed the garden. To the right was a heavy red leather-covered door which clearly led to the chapel. From behind them there came the sound of raised voices. The angry greenhouse man was attempting to stop the importunate fat man from mounting the stairs. The fat man appeared to be winning.

Theodora thought about dashing for the car. But this would have meant crossing the lawn at the back and they could be seen from the window of Makepeace's room. She hesitated but a moment, then drew Lucy through the chapel door and closed it behind them. The chapel was dark. It had, perhaps, been the dining room of the original house. At the far end, the sanctuary lamp glowed. Writhing pale plaster shapes of the stations of the cross emerged from the darkness as their eyes grew accustomed to the gloom.

Behind them came the sound of heavy footsteps. There was a smell of old candle grease, dust, wood polish, brass polish and incense. The footsteps got louder. Theodora glanced at Lucy, then took her by the hand. At the east end was an altar with a reredos which looked as though it had been copied from something nineteenth century and Italian. Swiftly the two women made their way up the nave. Hastily both genuflected and, as one, they dived under the altar cloth.

'There are too many people missing,' said Spruce, pushing his notes around in Harries Bar at six p.m.

Theodora looked guilty.

'For example, Sir Randolph Trimming has just rung to say that his son hasn't returned from his last night's constitutional.'

Theodora nodded. 'I think he may be—'

'Martin Guard and Sentinel are not at home. Where are they? That little beggar Jason with the red hair like a devil has absconded. I can't think why I didn't clap the lot of them in irons and just keep on working on them until someone told the truth.'

'They would have in Tibor's country,' Theodora agreed.

'Ah, so you know about Tibor.'

'I guessed he might be part of the goods trade run by Adjumentum Salvatoris.'

'I'm beginning to hate the sound of those words.'

'Look, I'm really awfully sorry about this,' Theodora tried again, 'and I ought to have, that is, I meant to mention it earlier but I know where Joshua Makepeace hung out. I mean both places.'

Spruce gave her a long look. 'First we can't find any address for him and now you say you have two.'

'He has a boat.'

'*The Admiral Hardy* and *The Pike.*'

'You know them?'

'No. Our Customs' Officer contact knew both the father and his son's boats.'

'So you haven't searched them?'

'*The Admiral Hardy* has been gone over by our people. They haven't found anything which would help our investigation. *The Pike* we can't find.'

'Well, it just so happens I did actually run across *The Pike.*' Theodora was genuinely apologetic. Poor Spruce was having a bad time. She had not been entirely fair.

'Local knowledge?' Spruce was bitter. *He* was a local man. Theodora had merely come down for holidays as a child.

She nodded. 'Do you know Drain Dyke by any chance?'

Spruce reflected. 'You couldn't get a boat of any draught in. It's been silted up for years.'

'I wondered if that might not be the case. In fact I think it may have been dredged within the last eighteen months. *The Pike* is lying at the north-east end. If you didn't know the spot you probably wouldn't find it.' She did her best to let him off lightly.

Spruce was not to be comforted. 'So you went?'

'Yesterday, before supper at Wrackheath.'

'And you found?'

Theodora pushed the two files across the table. Silently Spruce opened the first and glanced at its contents. 'A sermon?'

'Yes. I think Joshua wrote it. It's his handwriting, the same as on the sketch map from Holland, if you remember.'

'Have you read it?'

'Yes. I'm always interested in sermons,' Theodora admitted.

'And does it bear on the case?'

'I wouldn't say so. It shows he certainly cared about the Church. But then we know that from his membership of Adjumentum Salvatoris. It's really the other one I thought *you* might be interested in.'

Spruce smoothed out the ivory-coloured sheets of the second folder and began to read. A look of bafflement spread across his face. 'I don't read Spanish,' he objected.

'My own's not very good.' Theodora was as ever self-deprecating.

'So what is it?'

'I took it to be a form confirming the release of Joshua Henry Makepeace from Caracas prison in July 1977.'

'And the other bit of paper sets out his sentence eighteen months earlier.' Spruce may not have been a linguist but Theodora credited him with good inferential skills.

'What was he in for?'

Theodora leaned forward and tapped the operative word. '*Droga.*'

'Drugs? He was a runner, a pusher?' Spruce tried the labels out like new clothes. 'I can't believe he *took* them. Our forensics would have found some trace in his body. And he looked very fit.'

'He got out of prison earlier than he should, if you look.'

'Interpret,' Spruce said.

'There was a *multa*, a fine paid in order to get him released early.'

'Outrageous,' said the pillar of the British justice system.

'And you'll note it was paid by—'

'My favourite organisation.'

'So the question is, is Adjumentum Salvatoris running drugs or just getting poor unfortunates out of prison who might be unjustly treated?'

'Tibor,' said Spruce, 'tells us that he was picked up from his Hungarian prison by what he calls "The Fathers" and brought over here and housed and set up by them.'

'Was he drugging?'

'He says he was put inside for injudicious remarks about the government.'

'Could you check?'

'We've already set about it. But we don't have any Hungarian speakers in the Medwich force. We're going via London and it takes for ever – even if their records are in good nick and truthful, and if they'll release them to us.'

'So given what we know so far, how do you read all this?'

Spruce started to draw concentric circles on his notepad. 'Makepeace comes out of the Navy in '76.'

'Where he knew Martin Guard.'

'Right. He disappears from England and keeps in touch with his dad by having someone phone him every so often.'

'Sometimes Guard.'

'Right.'

'According to the papers you've found he was in prison for drug offences in South America and he was got out early as a result of the payment of a fine by Adjumentum Salvatoris.'

'Aka Guard,' Theodora finished for him. 'And the other figure who is prominent in AS in this area is Father Raymond Sentinel.'

'How do you know he was a member?'

'Lucy Royal found a copy of the Society's handbook and membership list in Father Martin's chalet.'

'What on earth was she doing there?'

'Seeking an entry into AS, I would guess?'

'Why?'

'Lucy is a dedicated supporter of African causes and she'd like to tap into a well-organised and apparently well-resourced structure to help her relieve some of her own protégés.'

'And you reckon AS is well resourced because of the drugs connection?'

Theodora thought how very much she did not want to come to this conclusion. She nodded. 'There is another bit of evidence pointing that way. I told you I'd visited both of

Makepeace's boltholes. The other one was at the HQ of Adjumentum Salvatoris in Felixstowe. Lucy and I went there this afternoon and we found these in the bottom drawer of Makepeace's chest.'

Carefully Theodora drew out the boots from Lucy's plastic bag and laid them on the table. Spruce took them up and repeated the tests which Theodora had tried earlier. 'The caps are carriers,' he concluded after a bit.

'The other thing you ought to know,' Theodora went on, 'when Lucy and I were at AS HQ this afternoon we met someone who was looking for Makepeace.'

'Who?'

'I've never seen him before.'

'How d'you mean "met"?'

'Well, more avoided really. We thought it prudent to withdraw to the chapel for a while so as not to get in the way.'

'Why?'

'He smelled dangerous.'

'What did he want?'

'He wanted to get to Makepeace's room.'

Spruce contemplated the row of brown boots on the table.

'I don't know.' Theodora answered his unspoken question. 'He might have been looking for them, I suppose.'

'He wasn't a priest?'

'He was not,' Theodora said firmly.

'I wish you'd talked to him or followed him or something.'

'There are limits,' Theodora protested.

'Yes,' said Spruce. 'But all the same.'

'So can we fit Makepeace's murder into all this?' she inquired.

'If he either is or once was mixed up with drug-trading then there could be a multitude of people who might want to kill him.'

198

'What about the most obvious?'

'Tibor?'

'He knew the organisation, only he called it the Fathers. He had Makepeace's picture in his wallet; he was out of the kitchen at the time when the murder was committed. But . . .'

'He didn't take drugs, has no record in pushing them, says he didn't ever meet Makepeace.'

'And the weapon and his coat have his own blood on them not Makepeace's.'

'So who would you put next?'

Spruce considered for a moment. 'It is obvious that Guard must be a suspect . . . He was probably bringing in people on a regular basis if he was the sailor who "knew a lot about boats" and brought Tibor in.'

'Lucy thought she heard him bringing in some Umundese on Tuesday night.'

'Who?'

'Very sophisticated and highly Christianised East African country north of Nigeria.'

'How does she know this?'

'She heard the sound of the language being spoken and Guard talking to them. And on Thursday when she was having tea in the room above here, she saw Guard make his way out through the wire in what she inferred was a well-worn path.'

'That fits in with what your uncle, sorry, cousin said at Wrackheath.'

'That the AS bring people in and stack them either at the Fathers' house, the Old Rectory, or in the attics of Wrackheath. Where would that place Nick, would you say?'

'I did wonder if he was their driver?' Spruce ruminated. 'Tibor said a dark-haired youth drove him in a German car to his safe house – i.e. to Wrackheath.'

'Nick doesn't have a German car,' Theodora objected.

'If AS are as rich as you say they may have one.'

'Why should Guard want to kill Makepeace?'

'Any number of scenarios is possible with druggies. Say he wanted to stop the drugs side of things and Guard wanted to continue. Or the other way round. Say Makepeace wanted a share of the money and Guard and AS weren't for raising the price.'

'I can't tell you how I hate all this,' Theodora burst out. 'I really can't see priests thinking it was morally acceptable to deal in drugs.'

'Not even if it meant that they could continue to finance some sort of pastoral and rescue work amongst the oppressed?'

Theodora was surprised at Spruce's agile spanning of moral and religious categories. She sighed. 'Well, you haven't got any direct proof of Guard's having killed him.'

'Whose side are you on?' Spruce was a shade indignant.

'I'm on the side of the loser.'

'That being?'

'Makepeace. He's the victim.'

Spruce was pacified. 'So we need to find Martin Guard and then I'd like to have a word with young Trimming and see if he can help us to fit in the odd piece.'

'I think I might know where Nick is,' Theodora said.

'Well, this time I'd like to go with you,' said Spruce.

Nick drove his Meccano tool home and the handle turned as sweetly as though it were responding to its own key. He swung himself into the car out of the cold of the November evening. It was a large old Mercedes, its beige upholstery soft but firm, comforting him in his distress. He liked Mercs. They were heavy on petrol but dependable and comfortable. He always took a Merc if he had the choice. He'd said he'd pick Jason up outside The Buccaneer at half-seven and Jas would tell him what to do next.

Nick had seen the police arrive at Wrackheath the previous night. He'd watched as they took Tibor away. He knew then that he'd have to keep away for a bit. Tibor would tell them all about how he'd been driven by Nick to avoid the police at Bolly's and stayed in Wrackheath's attics. And Tibor knew Jason and the firm used the attics every now and again. Nick tried to remember what he'd got stored there. Heaven knew what else the police might find if they did a proper search.

Later he'd crept back to try and get his mobile phone and his post office savings book. The book represented the five thousand he'd got saved towards the endowment, to rescue the house. Nick didn't think anyone could get the money out without his signature but you didn't know with the police. Perhaps they didn't have to ask, perhaps they could just take. Some of the people he'd driven and sheltered in the attics told horrifying stories about what the police could do to you. But that of course was abroad. In the end he hadn't been able to get either phone or book because they'd left a policeman at the house and he'd made himself comfortable in the kitchen. So that was that. He'd had to use the public phones in spite of what Jason had always told him about it not being a good idea because they could trace you so easily.

Nick peered at the clock on the dashboard. He had an hour before he could get to Jason. He wanted Jason to tell him what he could do about the future. He didn't know quite what he had done that was against the law. Nick had some difficulty following what was against the law and what wasn't. There never seemed to be any rhyme or reason about it. Why, for example, were some people allowed into the country and some not? The people he'd driven were people at the end of their tether. They wanted a safe night's sleep and some food. Even the rather chancy hospitality of Wrackheath was clearly paradise to some of them. What was against the law in that? But Jason said the police were against it and Jason always knew about such matters.

Could the firm go on? Could he go on earning money by driving and sheltering? And if not could he do something else for them? He'd told Jason about how he needed to earn money. He'd told him all about his plans for the house and how he needed to get an endowment. He thought Jason understood all right, at least about the money bit. And he knew the firm had lots of interests. Jas had said it was a really big outfit, world wide. Perhaps they could send him abroad for a bit. That would be OK with him, provided he could come back to the house when he'd made his pile. Surely they could use him somehow. He didn't mind much what he did.

At a quarter past seven, Nick did his trick with the Meccano part and turned the engine over. He was lucky. There was a full tank. He turned the heater up to its limit, switched on the headlights and swung her out into the late evening traffic. Nick had never taken a driving test. He'd never seen the need; he understood to get a licence you had to fill in a lot of forms and things and the firm had never asked him. It had never occurred to him you needed to learn how to drive, he felt he'd been born knowing.

The Buccaneer at seven-thirty was filling up with those workers who couldn't face home without a drink but it wouldn't get really busy till nine when the music started. Nick swung into the car park and found the spot under the trees where Jas liked him to park when they used the van. Then he switched off the lights and kept the engine running for warmth. He must have slipped into a light sleep because the next time he looked at the clock it was half past eight and the car was stuffy with the warmth. Normally Nick could spend hours with his eyes glazed in a sort of suspended animation. He didn't mind waiting at all. It made him a good driver, Jas had said, not nervy, didn't draw attention to himself. Apparently this was a good thing. But now he was beginning to worry. It wasn't like Jas to be late. He wound the window down and looked round the car park. It had filled up a bit but there was no sign of Jas. He wished he had his mobile and could press the magic buttons which would put him in touch.

The sound of the back nearside door opening suddenly took him by surprise. He smelled Jason's hair cream and heard his voice. Before he could look round Jason slammed the door and leaned close to his ear.

'Move off slow.'

Nick obediently let in the clutch.

'Slow. There's coppers by the entrance.' Nick saw the marked police car parked without lights but with a driver at the wheel.

'What's up, Jas?' he ventured as they turned out into the road.

'We go' a bi' of bovver, 'aven't we?'

'What sort of bovver, Jas?'

'Tell you in a sec. Take next left and do a U.'

'Why, Jas?'

'Case they fink o' follerin'.'

There was no need to ask who might be follerin'. Nick swung the car round. 'Where now?'

'Docks. Felixstowe Docks West Passage. Quick as you can but not so's to ge' done.'

'Why we going there, Jas?'

''Cause they're on to us, that's why.'

'Who's "us"?'

'Dave the Merc, me, the whole firm.'

'Me?'

'I spec' so. You 'aven't done much tho', just driven a few cars, like.'

'What have you and Dave done, Jas?'

'Not me, mate. Dave and the managers. They done it.'

'What they done, Jas?'

'They killed that bloke.'

'Which bloke?'

'That clown bloke. Vicar or wha'ever.'

'Why they kill him?'

'He didn't like it.'

'You mean he didn't like us bringing in all these people from abroad?'

'Wasn't that. He din't mind that, I don't fink. It was the other stuff.'

'What other stuff?'

'The stuff what made the money.'

'What was that?'

'The white stuff.'

Nick had a flash of intelligence, then a sinking feeling. 'Heroin,' he said, and in using the term showed how far he was from the real world of crime.

'Well, whatever they want really,' Jason said without interest.

'I didn't know they came in with that stuff.'

'Only some did. The ones who could get it past safely.'

'Which would they be?' Nick kept asking questions because he was wondering what to do. He'd never realised that the people he was ferrying were not some sort of refugees whom no one could surely object to having in the country. They brought in stuff with them.

'The ones the Favers gave the word for.'

'Which Favers?'

'Like I say, the clown-vicar, like.'

There were times when Nick failed to follow Jas. 'Do I know him?'

'Dunno.'

'What you want to use vicars, Favers, for?'

'Well it's good innit? See, even if they ge' picked up, like, who's gonna care abou' a set of 'gees looked after by the

Favers?' This was a long sentence for Jason, Nick recognised.

'So why you kill the clown-priest, vicar?'

'Me? I din't kill nobody.'

'Who then?'

Jason looked furtive. 'Dave said he was going to put a bi' of a push behind another Fave.'

'What, to kill the clown?'

'Right.'

'Which other Fave?'

'Dunno.'

'Why should one priest kill another?' Nick reverted to his own diction.

'He go'a do what Dave tell him or else.'

Nick got the general picture. 'So how the police know all this?'

'George the Forge give it away, din' 'ee?'

'Who's George the Forge?'

'He done the papers, like, the documents.' Three syllables took time with Jas. But he got there in the end.

Nick was speeding up. 'You mean passports and things?'

'Right. He's really, really clever is George.'

'So why'd he give the game away?'

'Four years's a long time for a man. He go' a wife and grandkiddies. He's a real family man's George.' Jason's sentiments did him credit.

'You mean he fingered Dave the Merc for some remission?' Nick had been in jail, he knew the trading.

'That was a really, really stupid thing to do,' Jason said heavily. 'Dave, he won't forget and he's not a forgivin' sort of man.'

'So where are we going now?' Nick asked.

'Right here and down by them cranes.'

The amber and white lights of the dock were hazy in the cold night air. The police patrol boat cruising round the west pier swivelled its beam over the uneasy water sweeping from north to east. In the background Theodora caught the sound of a hopper purring and the quiet clank of the conveyor belt feeding it. She was aware of there being more police in the area than Spruce and herself. They had parked in the compound where she thought she recognised two other unmarked police cars which had been down at Bolly's.

'Docks have changed since my youth,' Spruce said.

'Fewer people, more machines?'

'Cleaner.'

'Where's Edgecombe and Makepeace's Office?'

Spruce nodded towards the dark shape at the end of the dockside. 'Where do you think Jason and young Nick hang out?'

'Nick spoke of warmth, so possibly the boiler room or basement.'

As they neared the building, the sound of the patrol boat's engine got louder. 'Is that one of us?'

'I had a word with Marriot,' Spruce admitted. 'And of course the tides are just right.'

'As on Joshua's sketch map? They surely are not going to try and run anything or anyone in tonight? I mean after the murder?'

'Well, we shall see, shan't we? Martin Guard struck me as not likely to be put off his stroke by a small matter.'

'You think Guard killed Makepeace?'

'As I said, his prints are all over Makepeace's hollow-toed boots.'

'But I thought you said that your forger man didn't know anything about Guard.'

'George said he'd never *met* him. His contact was Dave the Merc.'

'Is this the way in?'

Spruce edged between a pile of pallet boards. 'I think we'll use the front door even if the others don't.'

He shook out keys and they entered the deeper darkness of the building. There was a smell of damp boots. Theodora felt rather than saw a staircase rising at a steep angle out of the small hall. Two storeys above them was a faint outline of skylight.

'Up or down?'

Spruce touched her arm. 'Listen.' She heard nothing. Then in the silence the sound of moaning. It came from the room directly above them on the first floor. Spruce began to mount the stairs. When he reached the door he listened again, then cautiously he opened it. Outlined against the light from the wall-length window could be seen the figure of a man, his head slumped on the table. He was bundled up in a duffel coat, his head concealed in the hood. For a moment Spruce was indecisive and at that moment came the sound of a powerful car engine.

'Lights,' said Spruce and Theodora flicked the switch. The room came shadowly to light with a single forty-watt bulb suspended over the head of the slumped figure. Spruce gently took back the hood. Martin Guard's head rolled back to disclose a knife in his windpipe.

CHAPTER ELEVEN

Envoi

'Keep up, everyone,' Chris Teane bellowed through the megaphone. The final act of worship of the conference had begun. Everyone agreed it had been a memorable conference. 'A fantastic experience,' the Evangelicals assured each other. 'A valuable opportunity,' affirmed the Affirming Catholics. 'It edifies the Kingdom through the Church,' the Forward in Faith Catholics contributed.

The conference-goers had gathered in accordance with their orders on the beach below the promenade at half past eleven in the morning. *Sea Breezes for the Millennium*, it had been called on the notice board, so here they were, goodwill polished and at the ready. This was the first time many of them had been outside the barbed wire surrounds since they entered Bolly's five days ago. There was a feeling of prisoners released. The organisers had not quite read their tide tables correctly. The tide was on the turn by the time they assembled, instead of, as they had supposed, on its was out for another half-hour. Harold Worsted just knew someone would blame him for this. The sand underfoot was, therefore, beginning to fill up with water and those who had not prudently changed into wellies were likely to get their feet wet before the final moments. Some of the older members of the congregation, especially amongst the laity, who were unused to liturgical innovation, were not accustomed to being without a book of words to follow the proceedings. 'We don't want people fumbling with bits of paper,' Teane had declared. 'We need to leave room for the Spirit.'

The general idea seemed to be that they would process along the beach for the length of two breakwaters, or about a half a mile. There would be a pause at each breakwater to hear the Word proclaimed or to have a bit of uplift from appropriate people. The Bishop would have his slot at the last breakwater.

'I'm afraid we'll have to cut your contribution, Miss, er Theo,' the Bishop had said as he stumbled over her at coffee break in The OK Corale just before they set out. 'I find I've got to be in London by five, so we're cutting the last session. Bit of a relief to you, I imagine. Ha, ha. If you let Peach have a copy of your thing we can circulate it with the conference papers, of course.' Privately he felt it was better that way. He didn't want to hear what the woman had to say and he doubted if anyone else did.

Theodora looked him full in the eye and said, 'I see.'

This made the Bishop feel uneasy in a way to which he was not accustomed. He backtracked. 'Or of course you could have a couple of minutes at Sea Breezes if you'd like. A sort of envoi.' He laughed deprecatingly at this excursion into the literary. He hoped to Heaven she'd have the wit to refuse.

'Two minutes is all I need,' Theodora assured him. 'I have an envoi from our jester priest.'

The Bishop was startled. 'I wonder if that would be quite suitable, quite decorous' – he shot a glance at the Archdeacon – 'in the circumstances.'

'I'm sure we can trust Miss Braithwaite,' said the

Archdeacon. 'I knew her father.'

So here they were labouring through the wet sand with a strong east wind vigorously opposing them. The Royals walked with Theodora in the front of the contingent. Riders all, the three of them had worked out that it would be better to walk on sand which had not been cut up by a hundred other feet. Theodora looked back over the long crowd behind them. She thought she saw Spruce towards the back. Just the sort of decent thing he might do, she thought. He must be grateful to be clearing up his incident room and going home victorious. She wished him well.

'So who mixed up the Bishop's slides?' Arthur Royal inquired. His hearing, not his strongest faculty, was not helped by the roar of wind and sea and the murmur of other worshippers who were not sure whether they should be silent because it was an act of worship or whether it was allowable to talk because it was being held outside.

'I said, dear,' Lucy turned towards him and bellowed, 'Daniel Ripe mixed his bag up with the Bishop's and put some of his, er, private slides in thinking he was putting them in his own bag. Apparently they were the same sort of bag.'

'They ought to have distinctive bags, like ours.' Arthur Royal was complacent.

'How did they find out?'

'Apparently Daniel accused the Bishop of stealing his bag. Poor Peach sorted it out in the end.'

'It's a pity they don't—' Arthur began.

'Hush, dear, we're going to be spoken to,' Lucy admonished him.

It was true. Enough people had reached the breakwater for something to happen.

'We've come here to . . .' Chris Teane said. But the roar of the wind carried away his words.

'He needs one of those microphone things,' Arthur said.

'They don't teach them to get beyond the second pew nowadays,' said Canon Oldsalmon, secure in perfect, unforced diction and a delivery which never failed to reach the back of his large church without raising his voice.

'I believe we're going to sing a hymn,' said the Archdeacon.

'No,' said Lucy, 'I think it's going to be one of those choruses.'

And so it proved. The young men on guitars and drums set to with a will but an unamplified guitar is not a suitable instrument in a high wind on the East Anglian coast in November. Little was heard but the repetition of the name of the second person of the Trinity. Those at the back had not realised that the chorus was being sung and continued with their own interests. Later it became apparent that Chris was inviting people to make up their own prayers and 'share them with us'.

A mistake, Theodora thought. She could see the good idea that lay behind it. It was just that this was no proper setting for such a thing to take place. The organisers seemed to have no idea of the differences between occasions.

'It's like a phone-in,' said Lucy.

'I do think it was very odd of Martin Guard to give way to that man Bloomfield,' Arthur said as they started off again on their trek to the next breakwater.

'It's the money,' Lucy answered him with feeling. 'You've got to have money to achieve anything in this world.'

'But you and I never sought to get money like that for our mission,' Arthur objected. 'We would have thought the whole thing tainted if we had.'

Lucy slipped her hand into her husband's. 'Your faith is so much stronger than mine,' she said happily. 'What *I* found odd was the notion that David Bloomfield was the brother of that young man who lectured us on St John. Kenneth seemed so very knowledgeable. How could he have a brother who was such a thug?'

'Dave wasn't thuggish,' Theodora said. 'He had many of the same qualities as Kenneth: energy, perseverance, a quick eye for an opportunity. He just wanted different things out of life. If that involved killing two priests to preserve an excellent cover for a drug ring, he'd have no qualms.'

'I hate to think that what I remember best about Martin Guard was his jeering conversation I overheard through the chalet wall the first night we were here.'

'Better to remember him as someone genuinely caring about Christian refugees, people who had suffered for their faith,' Theodora suggested.

'I fear we are going to have another interlude,' said the Archdeacon.

And indeed he was right. They had reached the final breakwater. The halt and the lame were helped Christianly over it. Some of the older members wrapped their mackintoshes round themselves and squatted uneasily on its slippery, salt-smelling timbers and waited for whatever the clergy would do to them.

This time the wind had dropped somewhat. It was the Bishop's turn.

'I have been told what to say.' He got his laugh. 'Chris here, our chaplain for that most important part of the church . . .'

'Youth,' murmured the Archdeacon.

'Youth,' said the Bishop, 'tells me that what we need is a gesture. I will not call it a ritual, ha, ha, in case some of our high Church sisters and brothers take me to task. What I would like you all to take part in doing is . . .' he turned to Chris. 'What is it, Chris? Something with seaweed, you said.'

Chris came modestly forward and took his place alongside the Bishop. 'Fellow workers in Christ,' he said, 'I'd like you to join together with me now, all of us, together, and pick up a piece of seaweed. There's plenty about!' He laughed joyfully then continued. 'I want you to hold it in your hand for a moment and think. Then I want you to pray that this seaweed will stand for your hopes for the new Millennium of Youth in the Church.' The Archdeacon smiled grimly. 'Then I want you to cast it into the sea as a living sign that the sea may take it and bring to pass all that you pray for.'

'I distrust his theology,' said Canon Oldsalmon.

'Oh, I don't know,' said the Archdeacon, who had plans for his bit.

The execution was more difficult than the organisers had anticipated. There appeared to be less seaweed about than they might have thought. People had to spend time dividing the bits they had found with those less fortunate so that everyone had a bit when the moment came. Then there was the move to the sea and the casting forth. Some of the casters were old and lacked strength. Their seaweed lodged in the necks of those in front of them. Others who had been lucky and had long swathes of the stuff to throw found that the wind was against them and some of it was borne back to them.

'What *are* we doing?' Arthur Royal asked Canon Oldsalmon.

'I don't know what you're doing, but I'm returning to base.'

'I think,' said Theodora, 'I'm going to follow you.'

'But, Theo dear, aren't you going to tell us what Joshua said?' Lucy asked.

'He said,' Theodora answered, 'there's fooling and there's fooling. Fooling as talentless shambles, as here. And fooling as showing us Heaven, fooling as showing us that the values we have in the world of ego, ambition, dominance and manipulation, at whatever level of fatuity, are the opposite of the Kingdom of Heaven's. Not, I feel, a lesson we want to learn.'

* * *

They had all gone. Spruce had taken his computers and departed. Theodora had been down to the kitchen to say goodbye and thank you to Victor. He was touched.

'It's really, really kind of you,' he said gratefully. 'We do our very best and not too many actually take the trouble.'

'How's Tibor?'

'He's not so bad considering. He says his boils are much better. They're going to see if Immigration can be squared. So he's going to come back next week and do the next lot, Confectionery and Cracker Makers annual weekend conference. We haven't had them before.'

She wished him well and lugging her baggage behind her made for the main gate. Jason was not on duty. There was a woman, plump and girlish but serious in her first responsible post. 'You can't come out,' she said. Then she bethought her. 'No, that's wrong, isn't it? I got that wrong. It's "you can't come in", isn't it?'

'Possibly.' Theodora didn't want her to lose her nerve in her first day.

She edged round the barrier which the girl was not able to raise. She hadn't got the knack of the machinery yet.

On the other side of the exit she noticed a car door swing open towards her.

'Care for a lift?' Nick asked.

'Thanks. Whose is all this?'

'Mine,' he said proudly.

'Where'd you get it?' she asked suspiciously.

'Dad. Well, it was going cheap. Dave won't need it where he's going. He says I can start a taxi firm with it.'

'Won't you be joining Dave?'

'Your nice Superintendent Spruce seemed to think it might not come to that?'

'You'll need a licence to trade,' said Theodora, squeezing herself into the seat of the old Mercedes beside him.